"You can't make that kind of promise, Mitch."

Daisy ran a hand over her porch railing. "I might have to sell. There isn't a big real estate market in Rebel, Oklahoma. Moving forward, I have to be practical."

"Everything we've done in the last few weeks has been successful, Daisy. You can't give up now. We only have four weeks left."

She hung her head and closed her eyes. At the moment she had neither the energy nor desire to discuss the topic further. "Life should come with one or two guarantees, shouldn't it?" she murmured.

"Hey, hey, I'm sorry." Suddenly Mitch was at her side with an arm around her shoulder. "I didn't mean to stress you out."

When Daisy met his gaze, he was close enough to see the dark flecks in her blue eyes. Time stood still between them and for a moment he allowed himself to imagine the impossible. That somehow, some way he could have a future with someone like her…

Tina Radcliffe has been dreaming and scribbling for years. Originally from Western New York, she left home for a tour of duty with the US Army Security Agency stationed in Augsburg, Germany, and ended up in Tulsa, Oklahoma. Her past careers include certified oncology RN and library cataloger. She recently moved from Denver, Colorado, to the Phoenix, Arizona, area, where she writes heartwarming and fun inspirational romance.

Books by Tina Radcliffe

Love Inspired

Hearts of Oklahoma
Finding the Road Home

Big Heart Ranch
Claiming Her Cowboy
Falling for the Cowgirl
Christmas with the Cowboy
Her Last Chance Cowboy

The Rancher's Reunion
Oklahoma Reunion
Mending the Doctor's Heart
Stranded with the Rancher
Safe in the Fireman's Arms
Rocky Mountain Reunion
Rocky Mountain Cowboy

Visit the Author Profile page at Harlequin.com for more titles.

Finding the Road Home

Tina Radcliffe

LOVE INSPIRED
INSPIRATIONAL ROMANCE

LOVE INSPIRED®
INSPIRATIONAL ROMANCE

Recycling programs
for this product may
not exist in your area.

ISBN-13: 978-1-335-48801-5

Finding the Road Home

Copyright © 2020 by Tina M. Radcliffe

This edition published by arrangement with Harlequin Books S.A.

For questions and comments about the quality of this book,
please contact us at CustomerService@Harlequin.com.

Love Inspired
22 Adelaide St. West, 40th Floor
Toronto, Ontario M5H 4E3, Canada
www.Harlequin.com

Printed in U.S.A.

But this one thing I do, forgetting those things
which are behind, and reaching forth
unto those things which are before.
—*Philippians* 3:13

This first Rebel Ranch book
is dedicated to my father, Joseph P. Russo.
When I was a young child, he opened up the
world of books by reading aloud tales that
swept me away to imaginary lands. It was
this love of the written word that made me
dare to think I could write a book.

Thank you to my Wrangler Team for their
support and to those Wranglers who helped
me build Rebel, Oklahoma: Tracey Hagwood,
Dawn Leonard, Tonya Lucas, Jenny and Ryder
Beardsley, Trixi Oberempt and Heather Pickett.

Only a writer really gets a writer.
Tipping my cup of coffee to my friends S and S
for keeping it real.

Thank you to my hero, Tom, who supports me
every single day of this journey.

Finally, many thanks to my agent,
Jessica Alvarez, for helping bring this series
to life. I am grateful to my editor, Dina Davis,
for her guidance and patience.
Each book makes me a better writer.

Chapter One

Police chief Mitchell Rainbolt shook his head as he slid into the front seat of his departmental SUV and tried to remember why he was still in Rebel, Oklahoma, running a department with less staff than the Arrowhead Diner across the street.

With a glance at the clock, he confirmed the time. Ten o'clock on a Friday morning and he was off to check out a report of trespassers because his next in command was MIA.

Again.

Ever since Roscoe McFarland announced he was retiring in a year, he'd caught a serious case of don't know, don't care.

Mitch put the key in the ignition. The only thing saving his sanity was that his new hire, one Daisy Anderson, would start on Monday.

The Kendall property was five miles outside of town. Empty for years, the two-story home had fallen into disrepair. A shame, because when Mitch was just a kid and doing his best to keep track of his younger siblings, the Kendalls had provided a haven he could count on during the long months while his widowed father disappeared on the rodeo circuit.

He made the turnoff to the property and stared at a do-it-yourself moving truck in the gravel drive and a mini-van parked closer to the house. He couldn't help but notice the flower bumper sticker on the mom-mobile. A bright yellow daisy.

Not trespassers. Someone was moving in. Mitch slowly drove around both vehicles, assessing the situation.

The yard showed evidence of a recent mow, and the branches of the ancient redbuds that lined the drive had been pruned. Even the hedges around the pale gray clapboard home had been trimmed back. The place showed a glimmer of its old self though it needed a good paint job.

When a football sailed over the hood of his patrol vehicle, Mitch's foot automatically hit the brake. He glanced left and then right. A dark-haired boy about eight years old stood off to the right, eyes rounded, and a girl of similar age and coloring stood to the left, her expression wary.

Mitch turned off the engine and unfolded himself from the vehicle. He closed the door and scanned the perimeter a little more closely. Two more children, boys he'd guess to be around four and six, played on the grass beneath a big oak tree.

"Morning," he said to the oldest children. "I'm Chief Rainbolt."

"I…I…I'm Seth and this is my sister Grace."

"Pleased to meet you. Are your parents here?"

The children exchanged looks that Mitch couldn't decipher before the boy spoke up.

"Aunt D is inside."

"Aunt D. Got it."

Crossing the yard, Mitch stopped to further assess the house. Though the old place held a special spot in his heart, plenty had changed in twenty years. The reliability of the porch steps for starters. They seemed dubious at best. He tapped his boot on each step before putting his weight on them. When he got to the landing, a scream echoed out to him from inside the house. The screen door flew open, banged against the clapboard and a whirlwind of strawberry-blond hair and blue jeans burst across the porch and straight into his arms.

"Whoa, there." Mitch stumbled back down the steps to the concrete walk, managing to keep both himself and the woman upright as he grabbed the rail with one hand while his other wrapped around her waist. She smelled like sunshine, cinnamon and apples, an alluring scent that had him captivated.

"I'm so sorry," she breathed. "I saw a mouse." The woman blinked and disentangled herself from his arms. She blinked again, her jaw sagging and her face paling. "Chief Rainbolt?" she sputtered, blue eyes wide. Red splotches of embarrassment covered her cheeks as she stepped back.

Mitch did a double take. "Officer Anderson?" She looked the same as in the Skype interview except…well, different. During the interview, her hair had been tamed and pulled back severely. Now it floated long, loose and curly around an oval face. A scattering of freckles stretched across her cheeks.

He found himself staring at the beauty before him.

"Are you here on official business?" she asked.

"Your neighbor up the road called in a report of trespassers."

"What?" Daisy's blue eyes rounded. "I bought this house."

"No worries. Mrs. Shupe doesn't see too well." Mitch raised a hand. "She uses a set of fancy binoculars, but it can't be easy looking across the field with those redbud trees in her line of sight."

Daisy's mouth dropped open, and then she began to laugh. It was a sweet sound that warmed him from the inside out.

"Everything okay out there, Daisy?" a female voice called.

A mature, gray-haired version of Daisy Anderson appeared from around the other side of the house with a watering can in her hand and a redheaded baby on her hip. The woman's steel-colored curls framed her face in a short bob.

"Gran, this is my new boss. Chief Rainbolt, this is my grandmother, Alice Anderson."

"Ma'am." Mitch offered the woman a polite nod.

"Pleased to meet you, Chief." She placed the watering can on the ground and offered him her free hand. "I rarely go by ma'am. Alice will do."

He took her hand. "Yes, ma'am. I mean Miss Alice."

"Gran, would you please keep an eye on the kids while I chat with the chief?" Daisy asked.

"Of course. That apple pie has cooled. We'll have a little snack." Alice turned to Mitch. "Care for a slice of caramel apple pie, Chief? Daisy made it just today."

He looked at Daisy. "Pretty ambitious, baking a pie while you're still in the process of moving in," Mitch said.

Alice laughed. "Daisy's always ambitious. And she bakes when she's stressed."

"Gran!" Daisy's face was rosy with embarrassment when she turned to Mitch. "Baking is a constant in an often chaotic world. I'm sure the chief gets that."

Mitch nodded, silently enjoying the exchange between the women.

"About that pie?" Alice continued.

"No, thank you, but I do appreciate the offer."

A moment later all four children filed quietly into the house, followed by their great-grandmother who held the baby.

Mitch's eyes went to Daisy Anderson's left hand. No ring. When he looked up, the blue eyes were assessing.

"Welcome to Rebel," he said.

"Thank you."

"So you bought the Kendall place."

"Sight unseen, which explains quite a bit," she said. "Like the mouse who thinks I'm invading his territory."

"Where there's one, there's a dozen. A cat or two will eliminate your mouse problem."

"Good idea." She met his gaze. "Right about now, you're probably wondering how you managed to hire an officer who's afraid of mice."

"No judging here. We all have our issues."

She narrowed her eyes as though pondering his words, but said nothing.

"Looks like the place needs some work." Mitch nodded toward the house. "It passed inspection?"

"Mostly."

"Mostly?" He raised his brows.

Her gaze met his and she shrugged. "I waived a few things to lower the price."

Mitch's glance skipped from the weathered railing of the porch to the questionable steps. "Not important things, I hope."

"I've got a carpenter coming out to fix the necessary items."

He nodded and gave the house another slow assessment. "House has sad central air and a few ceiling fans, as I recall."

"We're putting our hopes on that sad central air."

"Ever spent a summer in Oklahoma?"

"No. I guess this will be a trial by fire, won't it?"

"Oh, nothing that bad. The good news is everything grows here. Accidentally drop watermelon seeds on the ground, and they'll have produced enough for a harvest before you realize it."

"That is good news since we have plans for a garden." She beamed. "My first garden."

Mitch couldn't help smiling at her response. "The kids called you Aunt D."

Daisy took a step away from the house, concern shadowing her face. "I'm their legal guardian," she said quietly.

Mitch did a mental recap. His new officer had five children.

"All of them?" The words escaped before he could stop them. Mitch knew he was doing a lousy job remaining impassive. Still, there was no denying that five kids were more than a handful. He knew firsthand as he had been the designated adult in a family of five children himself.

"Yes. All of them. Their parents..." She kicked at a stone on the ground with a dusty sneaker, and then met his gaze. "We lost my sister and her husband six months ago."

The pain he glimpsed in her eyes sucker punched Mitch and he swallowed hard, averting his gaze. It was too bad they had so much in common.

"I'm really sorry," he finally said, knowing the words were insufficient.

"Thank you," she murmured.

The silence stretched for a moment, broken by the giggles of children that spilled out from inside the house. The joyous sounds seemed to snap them both from their reverie.

"You're going to raise them by yourself?" Once again the words were out there before he could rein them back in.

"Don't look so horrified, Chief Rainbolt. I'm a law-enforcement officer with crowd management experience. I'm confident I can control a handful of children." She offered a little smile. "However, my grandmother is staying with us...for the summer, maybe longer." Her smile widened, and she shrugged. "Everything will work out. It always does."

Spoken with the bright optimism of youth. As he recalled from her job application, she was nine years younger than him. Which made him an old realist. Looking at Daisy Anderson, he felt even older than usual.

"Why Rebel?" he asked.

"Why not?" she returned with another shrug of her slim shoulders.

Why not, indeed? Mitch couldn't resist a look around the yard. Plenty of space for kids to be kids. Yeah, Rebel was a fine town to raise children. Her passel seemed well behaved. Maybe she had worked out all the details.

Perhaps everything *would* be just fine.

A moment later he couldn't help but nix that thought. Mitch knew only too well how raising a family could mess up the most carefully intended plans, which explained why he was still in Rebel. Yeah, it explained a lot of things.

"The children won't interfere with the job, if that's what you're thinking."

Mitch turned back to Daisy and offered a slight nod. Did the woman really understand the big picture? In the days when he played both mother and father to his siblings, it seemed each dawn brought a new crisis, and sometimes no matter how hard he tried, he couldn't avoid disaster.

He tucked away his thoughts, instead focusing on the here and now. All that really mattered was that thanks to the county funding, he had a new officer. A new officer his department needed badly.

"You can still start on Monday morning?" he asked.

"Yes, sir."

"Great. I'd like your transition to be as seamless as possible. The county has recently approved additional funding for the Rebel Police Department. I don't want to give them any reason to change their minds. My plan is for those folks up at the county offices to fondly refer to Rebel as a well-oiled machine."

"And is it?"

"Is it what?" he returned.

"Is the Rebel Police Department a well-oiled machine?"

Mitch could only stare, surprised at the gutsy question. No use skirting the truth. "Not at the moment."

"The population here is about seventeen hundred?" she asked.

"About is a relative word in these parts. The transient summer tourist population headed to Rebel Lake and Keystone Lake down the road is around ten thousand. It's a long time from May to September. Memorial Day was a week ago, and the fun has already begun."

"What sort of fun? I'm not familiar with tourist towns."

"Everything from noise to other ordinance violations on the lake. And where there are summer folks, there are summer teenagers. Not that I have anything against teens. There's talk that I used to be one."

Daisy's lips twitched at the comment.

"Teenagers seem to find new and unusual ways to bend, twist and otherwise manipulate the law without quite breaking it."

"Yes, they do." She looked up at him, her gaze thoughtful and once again, assessing. "When was your last day off?"

"I'm on call 24-7."

"That can't be good for your disposition."

Mitch jerked back slightly at the words. He found himself unreasonably annoyed at the astute observation.

Crossing his arms, he pushed back his shoulders before answering. A good offense was always the best route.

"Point of the matter is, Ms. Anderson, Rebel is growing. We've had a developer take an interest in our town and, this autumn, a big-box store is going in between here and Hominy. I need funding and I need the manpower... I mean, personnel. We've been short on both for too long."

"Then I guess I showed up right on time."

Mitch stared her up and down. For a little thing, she certainly could hold her own. And yeah, she was right. She had shown up at the right time.

That should be a good thing, but it sure didn't explain why his brain was waving a red flag between his eyes, fast and furious, while his gut answered that it was much too late for warnings.

Daisy opened the door and stepped into the kitchen. Her grandmother sat at the farmhouse table next to ten-month-old PJ who laughed with abandon as she slapped the tray top of her high chair with chubby little hands, causing her plastic plate to jump.

"I never get tired of her laughter," Daisy said. She smoothed the wispy red curls and pressed a kiss to the baby's cheek.

"Were you out there talking to your boss all that time?" Alice asked.

"No. I went for a walk around the property. It turns out we have blackberry bushes behind that shed," Daisy said. "A pecan tree, as well."

"Pecan pie and blackberry cobbler," her grandmother said. "I am so loving this place."

"And it looks like there's what used to be a small orchard of apple and peach trees farther down. Though the entire area is so overgrown that it will take forever to clean things up."

"We can handle weeds and grass, can't we?"

Daisy sighed. "Yes. Perhaps I should hire someone. My to-do list is out of control."

"Probably a good idea. No telling what else might be hiding in that long grass. Snakes and mice and such."

"Ew." Daisy shivered. "Good point."

Alice placed a bit of mashed apple on PJ's plate and then turned to Daisy. "I like your boss."

Her boss. The reason she went for a walk. Daisy cut herself a sliver of pie and slipped into a chair. She was emotionally exhausted after talking to Mitch Rainbolt. Yes, he was her boss. That alone was a reason to be tense. The man held her future in his hands.

On a more basic level, she'd seen honest compassion and understanding in his calm brown eyes. More than she'd expected from a jaded law-enforcement officer. But there was something more. Something she couldn't begin to define that left her flustered and tongue-tied.

Daisy wrapped her arms around herself.

"He's quite handsome, isn't he?" Alice asked.

"Huh?" Daisy looked up.

"You were off in another place, weren't you?" Her grandmother grinned like she had a secret, and Daisy immediately recognized the smile.

"I was, but nowhere near the location of your line of thought."

Alice laughed. "I wonder if there's more where he came from?" she asked. "I've been widowed a very long time." A thoughtful expression crossed her face. "Who knows? Maybe Rebel has more to offer than either you or I expected."

"Gran, seriously?" Daisy put her hands on her hips and assumed the role of the responsible adult in the family. "I have five children. The answer to my problems lies in prayer, not in tall, dark and handsome."

"Oh, so you did notice," Alice said with a chuckle.

"I'd have to be blind not to," Daisy muttered. "However, let me repeat. He's my boss and I need my job, including the health and dental coverage."

"The important thing is that you have peace about this move," her grandmother said.

"I do." Daisy nodded. "I have perfect peace about the decision."

At least she had before talking to Mitch Rainbolt. She'd put on a confident front, but self-doubt began to creep in when she saw the concern in his brown eyes. Would everything work out?

Daisy sighed and glanced out the kitchen window

toward the yard that stretched all the way to their nosy
neighbor's fence in the distance. This was what her sister's
children deserved. Green grass as far as they could see.
Trees to climb. Adventures to be had. Maybe, just maybe,
living in Oklahoma would help them remember the good
times, ease their pain and remind them all that God had
His hand on their tomorrows.

"I have peace about it as well, Daisy." Her grandmother
touched her arm. "I don't know what would have happened
if you hadn't stepped in."

Daisy blinked back emotion. The loss of her twin sister was still too raw. "Deb was more than my sister. She
was my other half. There wasn't a choice."

"You gave up everything," Alice continued.

"We're family. That's what family does." She wrapped
her fingers around her grandmother's soft hand. "You're
in this too, so clearly, you get that."

"No big deal for me. My place is now a vacation rental,
and I'll probably make a fortune."

"Gran, you left all your friends in Colorado."

"As you said, it's what family does. It's unfortunate that
your mother doesn't understand that. Nor your boyfriend.
You could have used the help."

"Ex-boyfriend." As for her mother, Daisy would neither defend nor accuse her. It was pointless and wouldn't
change a thing. Besides, Gran had her own opinions of
her daughter-in-law and always had, long before Daisy's
father died. It was a topic that was best left alone.

"I have you." Daisy smiled at the woman who had all
but raised her. "That's all I need. That's all Deb and I have
ever needed."

When PJ began to fuss, Daisy took the baby from the
high chair. She kissed PJ's soft forehead and snuggled the
child in her arms. PJ smelled like all that was good in the
world, mixed up with an undefinable innocence and purity.

"So, how was the pie?" Daisy asked, doing her best to lighten the mood. "I tweaked the recipe. Is it an improvement?"

Her grandmother raised a knowing brow. "Your apple pie is better than usual, and that's saying a lot because you are the best baker I know. Hard to believe you had any room for improvement."

"It's better than your pies?"

"Oh, my, yes! There was never a doubt that Daisy Anderson is the best baker in the family."

Accolades from her grandmother meant everything. Daisy broke off a tiny bit of golden crust and warm apple and popped it into her mouth, savoring the light buttery pastry. Yes, it was good. Good enough to open her own shop? Maybe. She released a small sigh.

That dream was on hold for now. The kids needed her steady paycheck, health benefits and the five-bedroom house that Rebel's lower cost of living afforded them. Someday, she'd chase her dreams again.

Someday.

The squeak of sneakers on the kitchen's ancient, cracked linoleum floor heralded eight-year-old Grace's entrance into the room. As usual, her dark hair was a tangle, the barrettes that Daisy put in this morning, long since discarded. "Aunt D, we're bored. May we watch television?" Her twin brother Seth stood behind her, eyes expectant.

"Television is for kids who don't have all of this," Daisy said, with a nod toward the endless yard outside the window. "There's a bucket in the back of the van and a couple of pairs of gardening gloves. You two can go behind the shed and check out the blackberry bush I found."

"Aunt D? Really?" Seth interjected. "We're missing our favorite show."

"Television shows are not going anywhere." She smiled

at the duo, so much like their father. Tall and slim with hair straight as a stick.

Grace, always the drama queen, groaned as if in pain.

"Tell you what. If you fill the bucket, we can go into town for pizza tonight, and then we'll all watch a movie and make kettle corn."

"Pizza?" The twins echoed the revered word at the same time.

Daisy nodded.

The two headed outside, jabbering away and finishing each other's sentences. Daisy and her sister had been like that. Even more so as identical twins.

"Do you think it helps that I'm the mirror image of their mother?" Daisy asked her grandmother. "Or maybe I'm causing them to rip off the Band-Aid again every single day?"

"I have no idea. Sometimes life just plain stinks, and yet kids are much more adaptable than we give them credit for. They need the love, security and consistency that you are providing. So stop overanalyzing."

"Sam woke up last night with another nightmare," Daisy said. She glanced into the living room where the four-year-old and his six-year-old brother, Christian, stacked blocks on the oak floor.

"Daisy, give them time. It's only been six months. Sam is four. He's in that stage between being a little boy and still being a baby. For him, I think it may be a blessing that you look so much like his mother."

"Was it the right thing to move them from Denver? Away from everything they know."

"Away from the pain." Alice sighed. "You needed to move as much as they did. It does no good to keep rehashing this every five minutes. Stop thinking about the past."

Daisy traced her finger along the battered farmhouse table she'd picked up at a thrift shop. "What should I think about? How much work this house needs?" Daisy waved a hand around, taking in everything from the peeling wallpaper to the lopsided light fixture, and the olive green dishwasher that didn't work.

"That's all fun stuff," Alice said.

"Fun." Daisy stretched. "Tell that to my back. We've spent the last few days unloading that truck, unpacking boxes and getting this old house in shape. Yet, there's still so much to do."

"That's part and parcel of being a homeowner, Daisy. Besides, there's no rush. This is your home now. The good Lord got us here. He's not going to abandon us."

"Yes. You're right. I'm letting my tired muscles get the better of me."

"I'll put on a fresh pot of coffee."

"Wait. Did you hear that?" Daisy straightened, ears perking at the sound of tires crunching on the gravel drive.

"Aunt D, that policeman is here again," Seth called.

Mitch Rainbolt was back?

"Uh-oh. This can't be good," Daisy murmured. She handed PJ off to her grandmother and hurried to her feet and out the door. When the screen door slammed against the house behind her, Daisy cringed.

Relax, she told herself and slowed her gait to a casual stroll as she moved across the yard, while pushing her wild mane away from her face.

Again, she was struck by how he seemed to command the surrounding space. And from what she recalled about the embarrassing moments in his arms, the man was 100 percent muscle. Hair the color of warm chocolate peeked out from beneath his gray Stetson. As he approached, she could see that he held an animal carrier.

"Chief, did you forget something?"

"No, I brought you something."

"Is that a…cat?" she asked.

He held up two fingers. "Two."

Daisy stared at him for a moment, touched speechless by the kind gesture.

"Turns out Rebel Vet and Rescue has an overflow of kittens this time of year," he continued. "These are from the same litter. Eight months old. They've been spayed, neutered and vaccinated courtesy of my third brother, the vet."

"Just how many Rainbolt brothers are there?"

"Several. Plus a sister." He nodded toward the departmental SUV. "I've got supplies in the vehicle."

"Supplies too? That's awfully generous."

"Is it?" He raised a brow. "Or maybe it's the vet's way of ensuring that you become a loyal customer."

Daisy chuckled. "In that case, I'd say he's a savvy businessman."

Mitch set the carrier on the grass and opened the top. With the first sounds of mewing, Daisy's nieces and nephews and her grandmother appeared, eager to see what was going on.

"Kittens," Seth said, peering into the carrier. Both had white and black patches with white boots and predominantly black faces. "Are they twins, like me and Grace?" He smiled, his face more animated than she'd seen since they had arrived in their new home.

"You're right. These two are brother and sister," Mitch said. "One has a white nose and the other a black nose."

Once Daisy sat on the ground, it didn't take the animals long to climb right out of the carrier and into the grass. The one with the star-shaped patch on its nose head-bumped Daisy's hand, seeking attention, while the other waddled toward Mitch.

"Oh, my, they're so friendly," she said.

Mitch gently picked up the kitten who'd valiantly attempted to crawl up his leg and placed it back on the grass.

"Whose are they?" Grace asked.

"It looks like they're ours. Chief Rainbolt brought them," Daisy said.

"A housewarming gift," he said gruffly. "They'll keep mice out of the house."

"Well, Mitch, that was sweet of you," Alice said.

"I probably should have asked first," he murmured.

"Nonsense," Alice said. "This is exactly what the children need right now. Thank you."

Mitch met Daisy's eyes as he answered her grandmother. "You're sure I didn't jump the gun?"

"Gran's right. This is perfect. Thank you."

He gave a short nod.

Sam and Christian wiggled to the front of the group until they were closer to the carrier.

"What are their names?" Christian asked.

Daisy pulled little Sam to her lap before she looked up at Mitch.

"You get to name them," Mitch said.

A cacophony of excited responses sounded at the announcement as each child spoke over the next.

"Can I hold them, Aunt D?" Seth asked.

"One at a time and very gently," Daisy said. She turned to Mitch. "Thank you."

"I guess that means they can stay," he said.

"Oh, yes. Of course."

"Then you're welcome." Mitch nodded toward the drive. "Want to help me grab those supplies?"

"Sure." She put little Sam on his feet and stood.

Alice raised a brow and once again offered a mischievous grin.

"Stop that," Daisy whispered before she followed Mitch to the police vehicle.

Mitch popped the rear of the Tahoe and pushed his Stetson to the back of his head. Reaching into the vehicle, he handed her a bag of litter.

"Not too heavy?" he asked.

"Not much heavier than a ten-month-old," she answered. When their hands touched, Daisy jerked slightly at the brief contact and did her best to appear nonchalant. For a moment their eyes connected. Clear brown eyes with a golden hint searched hers before he looked away.

She couldn't remember ever seeing eyes quite that color before.

"Chief, this is...well, thank you. It's unexpected and really, your timing couldn't be better."

"Yeah, I figured." He grabbed several plastic bags from the back of the vehicle and placed them inside a litter box before he closed the rear window and liftgate of the Tahoe.

"You did?" She blinked, somewhat confused.

Mitch nodded "I don't want to get into your business, but I've been where you are. Not exactly, but close enough."

"Oh?"

"Trust me, Rebel will be there for you. I can guarantee that."

She stared at him, uncertain of what to say. While a part of her scoffed at the idea that anyone could possibly understand what she was going through, there was something about Mitch Rainbolt that said he was sincere.

"Cats aside, this town has a lot to offer kids...families." He paused, seeming to hesitate at his next words. "The Rebel Community Church has a week of vacation Bible school coming up soon. The town has a Fourth of July parade and festival. Later in July, the Rebel Ranch has a kids' fishing derby."

"Sounds like a great way to get city kids involved and feeling like this is home."

"True. *The Weekly Rebel*, our local paper, has a calendar of events."

"Thank you."

He lifted a bag in each hand. "This bag has wet food, and this one is full of supplies and a few toys."

"Thank you, again. I'm a bit overwhelmed by your generosity."

"Don't give me too much credit. This is all Tucker."

"Tucker?"

"My brother the vet." He looked at her. "You've got five kids here, and you keep thanking me. Are you really okay with adding two more to your bunch?"

"Don't even think about taking them back. This is the best thing that's happened to these kids in months."

He was silent for a half beat before his questioning gaze met hers. "Mind my asking how they lost their parents?"

"Car accident. My brother-in-law lost control." She took a deep breath. "Fortunately, the kids weren't with them."

A flash of pain crossed Mitch's face, and he shook his head. "I'm sorry for your loss, though I'm glad you and your family found your way here. This town has a way of healing the soul. I'll be praying for you and these kids."

Praying? Daisy blinked back emotion. Mitch Rainbolt was nothing like she expected. The interview had not prepared her for the man in real life. She dared to glance at his left hand. No ring. Which, of course, meant nothing. And really, why was she looking? No man in his right mind would be interested in a woman with five kids.

Just the same, she knew without a doubt that her new boss was dangerous to her peace of mind, and she hadn't even started work yet.

Chapter Two

The voices of reason were carrying on a fine discussion in Mitch's head Monday morning regarding the fact that he'd brought Daisy Anderson mousers. What was he thinking? The simple act bordered on personal, and he didn't do personal.

As he dumped water into the office coffeemaker, he rationalized the gesture as simply being neighborly. Mitch was the police chief. He'd have done the same for anyone new to town. Especially someone who was going to be working for him.

The internal conversation was still going on when at 6:30 a.m. the coffeemaker spit and hissed the last drops of a fresh brew into the carafe and the buzzer to the employee entrance of the station sounded. Mitch checked the peephole and let Daisy in.

Points for his new hire. She was early for her day shift.

He gave a mental nod of approval. Everything about the woman said professional. Although she was dressed in black slacks and a tidy white blouse, with her wild hair pulled back into a twist on the back of her head, he was still unable to avoid noticing how nice she looked. And awake. As if she'd been up for hours. With five kids, one being a baby, he supposed she probably had been.

"Morning, Officer Anderson."

"Good morning," she said, glancing around the small

police department office. "Sorry. I don't have my security badge yet." She inhaled deeply. "Smells wonderful."

He poured coffee into his favorite mug and nodded toward the pot and a stack of paper cups. "Help yourself to Rebel Roast. We have our own roasters in town. A pop-up shop that's here from May through September. Oh, and Henna will be here any minute with donuts."

"The desk officer?" Daisy's eye narrowed a fraction as if to ask, *Seriously?*

"Yeah. Her parents own the only donut shop in Rebel. Popular enough to be in business year-round. It would be an insult if I refused Eagle Donuts." Mitch shrugged. "Besides, she only brings them in on Mondays, and they're the best donuts in the county."

"Get 'em while they're hot." Henna pushed open the door and caught it with her hip while balancing a small bakery box on top of a large one. Dressed in a departmental gray uniform, her straight, black hair was trimmed to skim her chin. A wide, generous smile graced her face.

When both Mitch and Daisy stepped forward quickly to catch the door for her, Mitch's hand covered Daisy's.

"Sorry," he murmured.

"Thank you. Daisy, right?" Henna said with a welcoming smile. "Henrietta Eagle. But I go by Henna for obvious reasons."

"Nice to meet you," Daisy said. "Thanks for all the help you've provided getting my paperwork squared away."

"My pleasure. Great to meet you in person. I've got your uniforms in the back room, and your security badge and a few other things at my desk." The boxes wobbled. "Can you grab that top one?"

"Got it," Daisy said.

"That's for you to take home to your kids," Henna said.

Daisy's eyes rounded. "How did you know? I mean, about the kids."

"My sister works at the elementary school. Unlike me, she can't keep her mouth closed. I heard you registered three of them for school and one for preschool in the fall."

"Yes, but it's not a secret or anything," Daisy said with a smile. She opened the box and looked inside. "Donut holes. Thank you."

"Welcome to Rebel," Henna said.

Mitch silently observed the interaction. He'd known from the first interview that Daisy would fit right in. Then again, Henna got along with everyone. The last hurdle would be introducing her to his curmudgeon deputy. He glanced at the clock. Who was running late, per usual.

A half hour later, the door buzzed and then opened yet again. Roscoe McFarland stepped into the room. A Rebel Police Department ball cap that rested on the back of his bald head completed his uniform. The senior officer who bore a passing resemblance to the cartoon character Popeye nodded in acknowledgement when he spotted Daisy standing just inside the door.

"Roscoe, meet Officer Daisy Anderson," Mitch said. "Daisy, this is your partner, Roscoe McFarland."

Mitch wasn't sure whose eyebrows shot up faster—Daisy's or Roscoe's. He hadn't told either that they'd be riding together since the decision had only been made late last night as he mulled the fact that Daisy was the sole guardian to five children. No doubt both would not like the plan, but occasionally there were perks to being the boss.

"Not today." Roscoe adjusted his hat and grabbed a donut. He took a bite, chewed and swallowed before he met Mitch's gaze.

"Excuse me?" Mitch crossed his arms, looked pointedly at Daisy and then stared Roscoe down.

The senior officer had the good sense to appear embarrassed. "Beggin' your pardon, ma'am. Pleased to meet you." He turned back to Mitch and held up a bandaged thumb. "I've got an appointment to get my stitches removed. Then I'm headed to the county office to discuss my retirement portfolio."

Mitch took a deep breath, determined not to let the crusty deputy push all his buttons before noon. "We discussed this last week. If your appointments aren't on the calendar, they don't exist."

"I'm sorry, Chief Rainbolt, but my thumb and my pension are mighty important. I've got questions regarding my IRA and my insurance benefits that can only be addressed by a professional."

"Gallegos has already headed out to patrol the lake." Mitch shot a glance at the calendar and then to Henna. "What about—"

"No, sir," his desk officer said, reading his mind as usual. "He's on vacation until next Monday."

Nothing like being undermined by his senior officer in front of the new hire on a Monday morning. Mitch turned his gaze to Roscoe, clearly communicating his displeasure. Yeah, it was all downhill from here.

"Officer Anderson, you and I will monitor traffic in Rebel today," Mitch said. "We leave in fifteen."

"When he says fifteen minutes, he really means ten," Henna said. She nodded toward the back room, and Daisy followed.

"Been thirty years without a partner," Roscoe grumbled once the female officers left the room.

"I plan to use the wisdom of those years to get Officer Anderson fully acclimated to Rebel. For now, you're her field training officer."

Roscoe gave a slow shake of his head. "FTO? Bad enough you got me handling traffic citations and parking meters ever since that incident last year. Now you're sticking me with a new recruit," Roscoe said. He snagged a second donut before he turned and headed to the door. "I don't like it."

"You don't have to like it," Mitch said to his retreating form. "And she isn't new. Just new to us."

"Same difference," Roscoe muttered.

Mitch downed his coffee and poured another cup, re-thinking the decision. He was supposed to be up an officer when he hired Daisy. But with the information about her five children, he had amended his plans and the schedule for now.

His new officer had inherited a family. What would those kids do if they lost her? Images of his own child-hood flashed through his mind.

Nope. Mitch didn't want to find out. He had two other day shift officers who could handle the heavy tourist areas around the lake. For the interim, he'd keep Roscoe and Daisy working together and stationed where they were least likely to run into serious offenders.

Of course, once again that made him the relief officer. It was the only plan that would ease his conscience and let him sleep at night. All he had to do was keep them from figuring out what he was doing.

When Daisy entered the department lobby in uniform eight minutes later, Mitch offered a pleased nod at her spit-shined appearance. If only all his officers took such care in the details of the uniform.

"Why do you look like you have a question for me?" she asked as she climbed into the Tahoe's passenger seat and pulled the seat belt into place.

"Not at all. I was just noting that a twenty-pound duty belt doesn't seem to slow you down." He fastened his own seat belt and looked at her. "Did Henna provide you with the information and password for the online training web-inars?"

"Last week. It's been reviewed twice and completed."

He blinked. "*Wait a minute*. This is your first day and you've already completed the training?"

"Yes, sir."

"It took half my department two days to figure out how to access the internet and register."

"Maybe they need computer classes."

"Yeah. I guess so." He shook his head. "You took the exam too?"

Daisy nodded.

Mitch looked over his shoulder, signaled and changed lanes. "The county requires an eighty percent pass rate, or a retake is required. After two retakes they'll recommend a class. It's free. No cost to the officer." He adjusted the rearview mirror. "It can be a challenge with the different county and city laws to keep straight, so don't feel bad if you have to retake."

"I got a one hundred percent."

"What?" His brows shot up. "I…um. Wow. Nice work."

"Is there something else?" she asked when he was silent for several moments.

"The firing range. You'll need to qualify yearly."

"Completed."

He looked at her.

"I passed. No worries."

"I wasn't exactly worried, though you did take me by surprise. I spend a good amount of my time around here herding cats. I hadn't realized that I've unconsciously lowered my expectations."

"After nine years in uniform, I'm accustomed to being underestimated."

Mitch jerked back. He'd insulted her when the truth was she was the most competent hire to come along in years. "Is that how it sounded?" he asked. "No offense was intended. It has nothing to do with you being a woman."

"None taken." She met his gaze, her eyes revealing nothing. "Tell me about Officer McFarland."

Mitch took a deep breath and released it slowly. "Thirty years on the job next summer. He tried retiring at twenty, but got so bored he asked for his job back. Now he's going to try again in a year."

"He has an issue with being my partner?"

"Roscoe has an issue with being anyone's partner. He's always flown solo," Mitch said.

"A partner after nearly thirty years. No wonder he's got his feathers ruffled."

"Roscoe always has his feathers ruffled. But think positive," Mitch said. "You've got the day shift. Come fall, you'll be home in time to pick up the kids from school and have dinner with them. Most new hires work graveyard for the first year."

"You're giving me preferential treatment?"

"No, ma'am. Think of it as a trade-off. You don't have the night shift, but you do have Roscoe."

"Which is more challenging, Officer McFarland or the night shift?"

Mitch's lips twitched at the question. "I can't make that call."

"And what about Henna?"

"Definitely not challenging."

Daisy stifled a laugh. "No. I meant, what is her role at the department?"

"Henna pretty much runs the place. She does a bit of dispatching, handles the administrative duties, including handling the chief of police. If you need something, she knows where to point you. During the school year, she also manages our school liaison program at the elementary and high school."

"That's a lot multitasking."

"Oh, she's good."

Daisy's gaze remained out the window, taking in the town as they drove up and down Rebel's patchwork of streets. "How long have you been in Rebel?" she asked.

"Me? I was born here."

"You've been in the department how long?"

"Too long." Mitch shook his head at the understatement. "Elected chief four years ago."

"You've never wanted to leave Rebel?"

"Sure. Lots of times. However, I'm known for my terrible timing." He released a short laugh. "I always figured it was the Lord's way of telling me that I belong in Rebel." Though being police chief hadn't been in his long-term plans when he'd started down this path.

Mitch's dash began to buzz. He pressed a button on his steering wheel to receive the call. "Rainbolt."

"Chief." Henna's voice filled the vehicle. "Reece called. Asked if you could stop by the ranch when you have time. He said to tell you that it's definitely not an emergency."

"Thanks. Officer Anderson and I will head over there."

"Roger that, Chief."

Mitch turned to Daisy. "Since I'm showing you around town, this is as good a time as any for you to see Rebel Ranch."

"Rebel Ranch?"

He nodded. "Owned and operated by the Rainbolt family. I'm pleased to say it's an integral part of the Rebel community."

"Your family owns a ranch?"

"The largest guest ranch in the county. My brother Reece runs the place." He was unable to keep the pride out of his voice. After a rocky start, Rebel Ranch was now a thriving business.

"You mentioned a couple of brothers and a sister."

"Tucker and Reece live here in Rebel. My sister, Kate, spends a lot of time on the road with the rodeo circuit."

"The rodeo. That's fascinating. I've been to the rodeo in Denver quite a few times during the stock show, but I don't recall seeing her name on the programs."

"You probably have and didn't know it. She's a rodeo clown."

Daisy's mouth rounded with surprise. "There are female rodeo clowns?"

"The Professional Rodeo Cowboys Association sanctions over six hundred rodeos a year. But there are only a handful of female rodeo clowns. That explains why you've never heard of her." He smiled as once again his pride took over. "My sister is one of the best."

"Good for her."

He nodded. Not adding that while he was proud of Kate, he worried about her safety too.

When Mitch turned onto the ranch drive, he caught Daisy staring at the elaborate metalwork that comprised the archway and gate to Rebel Ranch.

The sight of the ranch entrance against the clear blue, cloudless summer sky really was awesome. Seeing Daisy's reaction reminded Mitch that Rebel Ranch had come a long way from their humble but heartfelt beginnings. His brother Tucker often said that Mitch needed to stop focusing on the pain of the past and remember the good things from their childhood.

Trouble was, Mitch was the oldest, and he remembered things differently from Tucker. It was as though they had different childhoods. In a very real way, that was the truth. Mitch had been raised by their mother. The rest of the siblings were raised by Mitch.

"That's some view."

His gaze followed hers up ahead and farther down the tree-lined drive to a pond surrounded by a canopy of weeping willows. Ducks glided across the sun-dappled surface of the water. Beyond the pond, two barns rose up on the left.

"They have ranches in Colorado, of course. Lots of them," Daisy said. "But I have to admit, I've been a city girl all my life. This is my first visit to any ranch."

Mitch sneaked a look at the woman next to him. Her eyes sparkled and a smile lit up her face as she took in her surroundings.

"I guess I've sort of taken all of this for granted," he mused. "Though Rebel Ranch has grown since I was a kid. Evolved, you could say. All thanks to Reece. He's the businessman in the family."

"What was it like when you were a kid?"

"This was my grandfather's land. He ran a successful horse ranch."

"You were raised here?"

Mitch nearly laughed out loud. He grew up in a trailer on the other side of Rebel. "No. We visited my grandfather on the weekends. This wasn't even called Rebel Ranch growing up. This was my mother's daddy's ranch."

"Your mother inherited the ranch?"

"Not exactly. It's a long boring story. The local gossips would be happy to fill you in at the barbershop or the beauty parlor."

Yeah, pretty much anyone in town would be happy to talk about how his grandfather refused to let Mitch's father on his land, and the Rainbolt kids didn't inherit the ranch until both their parents passed.

Daisy swiveled in her seat, her attention now focused out his side window. "What's that?" she asked.

Mitch turned to see what had caught her attention. In the middle of the pasture yard, ranch hands were setting up tents. "They're getting ready for the first big ranch event of the summer." Mitch parked the vehicle and unstrapped his seat belt. "And now I know why my brother asked me to come out here."

Daisy opened her door and took a deep breath. "That smell. Horses and hay." The words were spoken with the wonder and awe of a child at Christmas.

Mitch smiled, trying to see the world from her eyes. Didn't work. He'd lived in Rebel for far too long. The next thing he heard was a plaintive cry of surprise as she stepped down from the other side of the vehicle.

"You okay?" he asked.

"I am, but my shoes will never be the same." She groaned. "These are new duty shoes too."

Mitch held back a chuckle as he realized exactly what just happened. "You stepped in something, I take it."

"Yes." Disgust laced her voice.

"My fault. I should have given you a heads-up. When you're on the ranch, always look before you step."

Daisy laughed and gave him a sidelong glance from across the hood of the vehicle. "That information would have been handy five minutes ago." She shook her head and wiped her feet back and forth on the gravel.

"Come on. There's a hose on the side of the house." Mitch waved a greeting to a few of the ranch hands while he and Daisy crossed the yard.

"What a lovely house. Is this yours?" she asked as they approached a sprawling stone ranch home.

"No. It's the main building for the guest ranch. Reece built the place. They've got a billiards table and a giant flat-screen television and such. The smaller ranch events are held there."

"Where do you and the rest of the Rainbolts live?" Daisy asked.

"I live in town. My brothers have built homes on the property."

"The guests? Where do they stay?"

"There's a half dozen guest cabins with first-class amenities down that path." He pointed to the right. "Occasionally Reece uses the second floor of the main house for VIP visitors."

Daisy followed his gaze down the path through the woods.

"Do you mind sitting on those steps and tossing me your shoes?" Mitch unwound a hose from the side of the house.

A moment later he swung around at the jingle of horse tack. His brother Reece, in jeans and a denim shirt with a black Stetson on his head, sat on an ebony stallion. Why was it that his brother always looked like a dime-store novel cowboy hero? Yeah, the number two son had definitely been first in line when the movie-star good looks were handed out.

"Don't you have somebody to clean up the horse patties around here?" Mitch asked him. "My officer ruined her shoes."

"Did she now?" Reece slipped from his horse and greeted Daisy with a megawatt smile. "My apologies, Officer…"

"Anderson," Daisy said.

Mitch did a double take. Daisy's expression hadn't changed. There was none of the usual female flutters and swooning in response to his brother's aura of charm.

"Officer Anderson, this is my brother Reece," Mitch interjected. "Reece, this is Officer Daisy Anderson."

"Pleased to meet you, ma'am." Reece removed a glove and offered Daisy a hand in greeting.

Daisy glanced at the soiled shoes in her hands and wrinkled her nose. "Um, probably not a good idea."

"Good point," Reece returned with a smile.

"You're the brother who runs the ranch?" she asked.

"That's right. I'm the handsome Rainbolt brother." He winked. "Just in case you were wondering."

Daisy chuckled at the bold assertion. "Your ranch is beautiful," she returned.

"Thank you. We're hustling to prepare for our summer kickoff this weekend. We've got a real old-fashioned hoe-down planned for Friday night."

"That sounds wonderful."

"It is, and consider this your invitation to join us."

Daisy hesitated to answer, and Mitch knew she was thinking about her children.

"Friday night's event is for adults. The rest of the summer is dedicated to families and children," Mitch added. "Good opportunity for you to meet the townsfolk."

She nodded thoughtfully.

When Reece took off his hat and put his hand on his heart Mitch wanted to groan.

"Ma'am," his brother continued. "I'd be insulted if our newest law-enforcement officer didn't join us."

Her brows raised slightly, and she smiled. "Then I accept your invitation, Mr. Rainbolt."

"It's Reece, and you just made my day." Once again he offered the full Reece wattage.

Mitch took a deep breath. His brother was on a roll now.

"There's a ladies' room inside if you'd like to wash your hands. In the meantime, I'll take those shoes and get them cleaned up."

"Oh, that's unnecessary. I'm sure hosing them off would be sufficient."

"Miss Daisy, you've got to let a cowboy be chivalrous."

Miss Daisy? Mitch blinked at the words, finding himself unreasonably annoyed.

"It's the way we do things out here," his brother continued. "I've got some good leather cleaners in the barn. Just take a jiffy. They'll be good as new." He nodded toward the guesthouse. "There's coffee on the counter in there. Help yourself."

"I, um…" She looked to Mitch.

"You may as well give in now," Mitch said. "Reece will pester you to death until you say yes."

She smiled and handed Reece the shoes. "All right, then. Thank you."

Mitch waited until Daisy was out of earshot, then uncrossed his arms and turned to his brother. "Kind of early in the morning for you to be spreading the malarkey so thick with my new employee."

Reece merely laughed and headed toward the barn with the shoes dangling from his gloved hands. "Wake up on the wrong side of the saddle?"

"Nope. What you see is what you get. Every single day."

"Yeah, and I'm still trying to figure out how it is you're such a curmudgeon when the rest of the family has magnetic personalities."

"Magnetic, huh? You're like a used-car salesman on a horse."

Reece only laughed at the words.

Mitch followed him into the barn where they both grabbed a couple of rags and saddle soap. They worked silently for several moments removing debris.

"I like your Daisy Anderson," Reece said.

"Glad to have your approval, but she isn't *my* anything," he fairly growled. As if a beauty like Daisy would be interested in a beast like him. Not likely.

"Interesting," Reece said.

"What?" Mitch asked, his annoyance doubling.

His brother shoved his Stetson to the back of his head and studied Mitch for a moment. "You like her too."

"Don't start." He held up a palm. "The woman is thirty-two years old."

"Age is only a number."

"My number is nine years older than hers, and my number is old." Never in his wildest dreams would someone young and full of so much potential, like Daisy, be interested in someone like him.

"Mitch, according to you, you were born old." Reece laughed. "I don't believe that for a minute."

"She has five children."

"Whoa." His brother's head snapped back. "What? Started early, huh?"

"Adopted her nieces and nephews."

"Ah." Reece cocked his head. "What's the problem? You like kids."

"I like Tucker's kids because they sleep at Tucker's house." Mitch shook his head. "We've discussed this before. I've already raised a family." And he'd lost one of his siblings along the way. Some parent he'd turned out to be.

"That doesn't count. You raised your brothers and sister."

"Yep. That's right and I'm not doing it again." He eyed the shoe in his hand and began to polish the leather. "Why was it you called me out here?"

"I'm short-handed for Friday night."

"How come you only call me when you need a favor?"

"Easy there, pal." Reece took the shoe from him. "You're going to rub the leather clean off."

"I told you last year," Mitch continued. "I'll help with the cattle and the horses, but I draw the line at people."

"You're the police chief. You deal with people all the time."

"Exactly." Mitch shook his head once again. "I thought Kate was coming home for the summer."

"She called me last night. Another opportunity opened up. She's headed to Oregon. Can't help it if our little sister is good at what she does."

"Good at what she does is fine, but it would be nice if she'd find a less dangerous calling."

"Don't start that again. You're proud enough of her when you see her on the television."

"This isn't about being proud of her," Mitch said.

Reece met Mitch's gaze. His brother's blue eyes bore into his soul. "It's been five years, Mitch. You can't bring Levi back by blaming yourself. You're not in charge of everyone's well-being. It's time to turn it over to God."

Yeah, right. They were the same words he'd been telling himself since his little brother died. It wasn't his fault. Except it was.

"Are you even listening to me?" Reece asked.

"Yeah. I heard you." Mitch rubbed a hand over his face. "So hire someone to cover for Kate. I can't work two jobs."

"I've got a guy coming down from Montana. Won't be here until Monday. I need help with the hoedown."

"Okay, fine. But this is the last time. I can't be a part-time cowboy when I'm a full-time police chief."

"This is the last time."

Mitch grumbled under his breath. "How many guests are we talking?"

"I'm booked solid." Reece dusted off his hands. "Thinking about expanding. Guess we can talk about it at the next family meeting."

"Sometimes it's better to stay small and in high demand than expand and dilute the quality," Mitch said.

"That so?"

"I'm just saying."

"I'll take that under consideration." Reece headed out of the barn. "By the way, Mr. Temporary Cowboy, the door is always open for you to work full time at the ranch. I'd like nothing more than a little help with the decision making around here on a daily basis."

"Not going to happen. I like my job."

"Do you? 'Cause the way I see it, being police chief isn't much different from raising children."

"The way you see it?" Mitch scoffed, annoyed that his

brother was spot-on in his observation. "You don't have any kids."

The sunlight greeted them as they walked out of the barn. "All the same," Reece continued, "if you worked at the ranch, you could toss those saddles of responsibility off your shoulders. Start enjoying life."

"You'd hate having me around all the time."

"Not true."

For a moment, Mitch considered his brother's words. He'd never imagined Reece would turn the ranch around as he had. The place was a success. There was plenty of work at Rebel Ranch, but could he be happy as a full-time cowboy? He'd always been in charge. Didn't know anything else.

"Can you at least pray about it?" Reece asked as though reading his mind.

"I can do that," Mitch said. He nodded as he spoke, and when he raised his head, his gaze landed on Daisy, who stood on the front steps of the guesthouse waiting. When her eyes met his, they widened a fraction, and a smile touched her lips.

Mitch could only stare, fascinated, as the breeze pulled a ribbon of curly gold-red hair loose from her tight knot and caressed her face with the strand.

At the same time, an elbow jabbed his side, pulling him out of his daze. Reece chuckled. "You're in trouble, and you don't even know it, big brother."

Mitch swallowed. It occurred to him that Reece had just said the exact words the voice in his head had been spouting all morning. He took a deep breath as he realized that there wasn't a single thing he could do about the situation except stay focused and keep his distance.

A drop of sweat trickled down Daisy's face. She swiped at her forehead with the back of her hand before rolling down the window of the patrol vehicle and waiting for the spring breeze to pass through the car.

The air was still.

"Mind if I turn on the air conditioner?" she asked Roscoe. "Seems a bit humid today."

The senior officer chuckled from the driver's seat of the Crown Victoria. "Help yourself."

Daisy rolled up the window again. She fiddled with the buttons, then leaned back in the cloth seats and sighed as the cool air touched her damp skin.

"Oklahoma in June," Roscoe said. "This ain't nothing. Wait until July."

She grimaced. "Really?"

"Oh, yeah. Sometimes the air's so thick it's like walking into a sauna with a sweater on."

Daisy pushed back a curly tendril of hair. Humidity. Her hair would love that. "I guess I'm used to Colorado's dry heat."

"Yep. Gonna be a long summer for you."

"Officers in the vicinity of Main and Drummond, please respond."

Daisy eagerly straightened and listened as the dispatch call from Henna echoed into the vehicle.

"Eighteen-zero-two, 10-4," Roscoe said to dispatch as he pulled on his seat belt. "We got this, Henna."

"Negative, 1802. Eighteen-zero-five is en route," Henna returned immediately.

Roscoe slapped a hand on the steering wheel. "That's the fourth time she's done that this week."

"I'm sure it's a coincidence," Daisy said.

"No coincidence about it. We're six blocks closer to that location than 1805. I know when I'm being stonewalled."

"On purpose?" Daisy asked. "But why? And by whom?"

"You tell me. The only thing I'm sure of is that I keep putting two and two together, and every time I get four."

Daisy tried not to smile at his words. Roscoe, she was

learning, had a flair for the dramatic, and most of the time his references made no sense.

"Does this have something to do with your retirement?" she asked.

Her partner released a loud snort. "My retirement? Now, why would you say that?"

"Maybe the chief thinks you've already retired."

Roscoe's head jerked around and stunned eyes pinned her. "'Scuse me?"

"This is Friday," she said. "You were MIA most of Monday and left early for appointments on Wednesday and Thursday." Daisy blinked as he continued to stare. Subtlety had never been her strong suit, and she'd already determined that Roscoe was a what-you-see-is-what-you-get guy. In the long run, he'd appreciate honesty. She hoped.

"Don't hold back now," he muttered.

"I'm only stating the obvious. It might appear to the chief that you've already checked out."

"Naw, that's only one side of the story. It's the chief who put me out to pasture. Ever since I saved that kid from drowning last summer."

"You saved a kid from drowning? Well done, Officer McFarland." She reassessed the man, realizing that there was more depth than she'd assumed to the officer sitting in the driver's seat.

"Oh, yeah. I'm a real hero," he laughed. "Read real nice in *The Weekly Rebel*. Trouble was, I nearly drowned myself. Spent a month in the hospital with aspiration pneumonia. Mitch was beside himself." He hung his head. "Went on and on about protocol. Truth be told, situation would have never happened if I had the common sense to close my mouth while I was doing the saving."

"So the chief is protecting you until you leave the department."

"That's my assessment." Roscoe nodded. "It's true, I've had a few minor mishaps lately." He held up his bandaged thumb. "But I can tell you the situation around here has gotten worse since you showed up on Monday."

"I'm sure your attitude has nothing to do with things."

"Ouch!" Roscoe shot her another surprised look before the stubbornness faded from his face. "I admit I've been a bit annoyed that he assigned me a partner."

"A bit annoyed. Until today, you've only spoken a grand total of three words to me."

"You were counting?"

"There hasn't been much else to do. Yesterday, when we were on break and accidentally collared that shoplifter in the Piggly Wiggly, I believe you said, *Cuff him, Danno.*" She couldn't help but smile. "Three words."

Roscoe chuckled.

Daisy kept talking since she had his attention. "The point is, this is my first time with a partner since I was a rookie with a training officer, so you're not alone. But I'd like to make this work."

"How many years you got under your belt?"

"Nine. And you?"

"Twenty-nine."

She raised a palm in gesture. "I could learn a lot from you, Officer McFarland. If you'd allow me to."

"Point take, Officer Anderson."

Silence stretched for several moments as Roscoe gnawed on a toothpick. "You know, there is another way to look at this," he finally said.

"What's that?" Daisy asked.

"Ever think maybe the chief has me babysitting you?" he asked.

"What?" Her eyes popped wide at Roscoe's words.

"I heard you've got five kids. Knowing Mitch's history, I can see him trying to protect you. That's his MO."

"His MO?"

"Let's just say the man has had more than his share of loss, and leave it at that."

"I see." Daisy said the words slowly, trying to gain insight into her enigmatic boss. "I think we should talk to him about our situation. I don't like the idea of being coddled."

"I ain't saying a word." Roscoe blew a raspberry. "Nobody likes a grumbler."

Daisy resisted the urge to inform him that he'd been grumbling for the last fifteen minutes.

"If they want to pay me to do nothing, it's no skin off my nose." Roscoe glanced at the dash clock. "Besides, why look for trouble on a Friday afternoon? The shift is almost over, and we've got a free meal prepared by the best chef in the county waiting on us at Rebel Ranch this evening."

"That event at the guest ranch? I nearly forgot."

"Well, don't. Everyone in town attends. Would be downright insulting to the Rainbolts if you were a no-show."

"Fine. I'll be there." She turned to her new partner. "I still think we should talk to the chief. Get things out in the open. Mitch seems like a man who favors transparency."

"Transparency?" He snorted. "It's transparent to me right now that talking to Mitch is a lousy idea." Roscoe signaled and checked his mirrors. "You do what you want, missy. Just remember you might not like the answers."

"Where are we headed?" Daisy asked.

"We've got two hours left. Enough time to check the meters on Main Street one more time. Who knows, maybe we'll run into some bad guys jaywalking and make a big collar." He laughed and pulled out into traffic.

Daisy adjusted her sunglasses and pondered Roscoe's words. Surely he was exaggerating. Still, a niggling doubt inched its way in and she was determined to prove Roscoe wrong.

Chapter Three

"What do you mean the funds are being withdrawn?" Mitch leaned back in his chair and shoved down the frustration threatening to erupt. He pinned his most intimidating gaze on the representative from the Osage County offices in Pawhuska. Will Needleman didn't even flinch. Trouble was, he'd known Will since they were kids. Hard to intimidate someone he'd gone fishing with every summer since they were old enough to bait a hook.

Will raised his hands, palms out. "Hey, pal, I'd appreciate it if you didn't shoot the messenger."

Mitch glowered at his old friend.

"Look," Will continued, "every small town in the county is begging for a slice of the discretionary funding pie. I've heard the same story everywhere I go." He adjusted his wire-rimmed glasses and clicked open his briefcase. "I can show you the numbers."

"I don't want to see the numbers. What I want to know is why you emailed me that the funds were approved for Rebel." Mitch pointed to his computer. "I have it in writing and now you're reneging. I am not happy."

"I'm not real thrilled myself," Will muttered. "Mushroom management puts me in the hot seat once again."

"Let me make the situation a little clearer for you." Mitch took a calming breath. "I've hired an officer based on your email."

Will stared at Mitch, eyes round behind his glasses. "That's not good."

"Not good? That's all you have to say?"

Mitch gripped his chair arms. Daisy Anderson quit her job and moved here with five kids. How was he going to tell the woman that there was a good chance he was going to have to unhire her?

"I, uh…" Will looked from the paperwork to Mitch. "You know this isn't my fault. Right?"

"What happened?" Mitch persisted.

"A few days ago, a memo went around that fund approval would now be based upon civic engagement."

"Who decided this?"

"I'm not privy to that information."

"Aw, come on, Will. You've worked for the county for a long time."

"I told you. Mushroom management. They keep me in the dark."

"You know everything that goes on, and this smacks of a politician up for reelection."

Will leaned closer. "You're correct. It's politics," he said quietly. "Everything is politics."

"They're playing with the funding for bragging rights?"

"Tangible results are what they're asking for."

"That's what I said," Mitch continued. "Bragging rights."

Will adjusted his collar and loosened his tie while at the same time Mitch clenched and unclenched his hands.

"What's next?" Mitch asked.

"I submit my recommendations August first and you'll know something shortly after."

"So I have, what, less than ten weeks to prove that Rebel deserves the funds and that our plan will make management look good?"

"Basically, yes."

"Between you and me, Will, our budget has about that

long to keep our new officer on staff. And only with some very clever math."

"I'm really sorry, Mitch, but I'm going to give you a little inside advice. Show the committee something they haven't seen before. That's the best way to earn that check."

"Isn't maintaining the law enough civic engagement?"

"Once again, this wasn't my idea."

"Civic engagement," Mitch muttered. The buzzword left a sour taste in his mouth.

"Here's the paperwork." He handed Mitch a sheaf of papers. "I've listed all the pain points for you."

"I'd like to show someone a few pain points," Mitch muttered as he assessed the stack of forms.

"Henna here?" Will carefully closed his briefcase and stood. He stepped to the doorway and looked around the main lobby.

"She probably left early. Tonight's the summer kickoff at Rebel Ranch."

"Yeah, I'll be there," Will said. He turned and faced Mitch. "Just between us. Do you think I have a chance with Henna?"

"A chance at what?" Mitch noted the earnest expression on the other man's face, and frowned when understanding dawned. *"No. Absolutely not."* He too stood, stepping around his desk and into the lobby, hoping to encourage Will's speedy departure.

"Really? I thought she and I were making progress."

"I mean, no, I don't want to discuss, contemplate or have further conversations about the personal business between you and any member of my department." Mitch narrowed his gaze. "Got it?"

"I, uh—"

The back door buzzed, and Daisy walked in. His newest officer had a bright smile on her face. She was having a very good day. Mitch grimaced at the irony.

"Happy Friday," she said.

"Yeah. Right. Officer Anderson, this is Will Needleman from the county offices in Pawhuska." Mitch nodded toward Will. "This is the new officer I was telling you about, Will."

"Oh?" Will turned to Daisy. "Oh! You."

"Excuse me?" Daisy asked as she shook his hand. Her confused gaze moved between Will and Mitch.

"A pleasure, ma'am." Will quickly started for the door. "I better be going."

"Good idea," Mitch said.

"Tell Henna I asked about her."

"Yeah, I'll do that." *When pigs fly.*

Daisy frowned. "Is he all right?" she asked as the door thudded closed behind Will.

"Probably not."

"Okay," she returned, looking more confused.

"Did you need something, Officer Anderson?"

"Do you have a minute, Chief?"

"As a matter of fact, I do not." He glanced at his watch. Right now he needed time and distance so he could figure out what he was going to do about the mess he had been sucked into.

"How about half a minute?" she returned.

A hopeful smile lit her face, and Mitch considered changing his mind. Then he remembered the corner he'd been backed into by Will and the county. It would take more than half a minute to explain what was going on. Yeah, if he was going to talk to Daisy about anything, he'd have to address the current situation, as well.

Not going to happen at six o'clock on a Friday afternoon.

"I'm thirty minutes late," he returned a little more gruffly than he intended. "I'm supposed to be at the ranch. Can it wait until Monday?"

"Yes, of course." She offered a wave of her hand in dismissal. "It's not life or death or anything."

When she stepped back and studied her shoes, Mitch felt like a complete jerk.

"I guess I'll see you tonight," he said.

"Yes," she replied with a short nod.

"Are you nervous about this evening?" he asked.

She shrugged. "Maybe a little."

"I've been through this every year since my brother took over the ranch. I can tell you that the ranch chef will make the event worth your time. So you greet and eat and leave. In and out and no one gets hurt."

"I can do that," she said, a smile returning to her face. "So you aren't much of a party person either, I take it?"

"Four years as chief and I still dread the whole being social part of the job."

When she met his gaze, her blue eyes warm with understanding, Mitch found himself unable to look away.

"That makes two of us," she said.

"I guess so," he said.

"Do you happen to know the dress code?"

"Dress code?" Mitch raised a hand and dropped it. "I, um…"

The door opened and Henna walked in.

"Henna can help you with that."

"With what?" Henna asked.

"Dress code for tonight?" Daisy asked the department admin.

"Jeans, denim skirt. Anything you can dance in and don't mind if it gets decorated with a little hay, red dirt and campfire smoke." She grinned and linked an arm through Daisy's. "Text me your choices, and I'll help you decide."

"Thank you, Henna," Daisy said.

"No problem. We gals have to stick together."

Daisy returned the smile and nodded. "I'll see you both later, then."

Mitch's gaze followed Daisy as she left. He ran a hand through his hair.

"You all right, Chief?"

He looked up at Henna. "I thought you were gone for the day."

"I ran weekly receipts to the bank before they closed."

Mitch offered a distracted nod.

"I saw Will outside." Henna crossed her arms. "Did you tell Daisy yet?"

Mitch's head jerked up. "Will told you."

"To be fair, I pulled it out of him." She sighed. "He was pretty upset."

"I'm not too thrilled myself. Things don't look good," he said. An ache settled in the pit of his stomach at the admission.

"How not good?"

"If we don't find a way to be first in line for those funds, I may have to let Daisy go."

"I was afraid you were going to say that." Henna closed her eyes for a moment as if to allow his words to sink in. "You need to let her know what's going on as soon as possible."

"I will. Just not until Monday. I'm not going to spoil tonight. It's her welcome to Rebel."

She lifted her brows and gave a slow shake of her head. "It won't be much of a welcome if Daisy finds out that she may lose her job."

"Yeah, that's why she isn't going to find out. Yet. You keep Will away from Daisy, and everything will be okay."

His admin frowned, a pained expression on her face. "As far as plans go, this doesn't seem to be your finest."

Mitch released a deep breath. Henna was right, and he didn't need the voice in his head to tell him he was a coward.

"What do you think?" Daisy asked. She stepped into the living room and did a pirouette to show off her new burgundy Western shirt tucked into the waist of the boot-cut jeans.

Her grandmother looked up from her spot on the couch between the children who were watching their favorite movie. On the floor, the kittens had curled into balls of fur and snoozed on a blanket. She grinned. "Look at you with those pearl buttons and corded trim. Ooh! Cowboy boots too."

Daisy struck a pose and lifted the hem of her jeans. "Nothing says city slicker like brand-new boots, but when in Rome. Besides, I already had one unexpected experience with ranch life. This time, I'm prepared."

The twins glanced up at her, and their eyes widened.

"Aunt D, you look like a real cowgirl," Seth said.

"Uh-huh, you do, Aunty Daisy. I like your braid too," Grace added.

"Thank you, guys. That means a lot."

"You need one of those hats like Chief Rainbolt wears," her grandmother added.

"A Stetson?" Daisy chuckled. "That might be pushing this cowgirl thing over the edge, Gran."

"Nonsense. Your birthday is coming up. We'll have to check into that."

Daisy shook her head. There was no stopping her grandmother once she'd made up her mind. The best path was to change the subject. She turned to the twins. "You'll be good for Gran while I'm gone, right?"

They both nodded.

She routinely asked them to behave, but she was very careful never to ask them to take care of the younger children. Daisy understood only too well what it was like to be forced to grow up too soon when a parent died. The twins deserved a childhood of their own, and she intended to give them one. She was determined to put the joy back into their lives.

"I hate that I'm leaving you with the kids again," Daisy said to her grandmother.

"Honey, that's why I'm here," Alice said. "It's important that you get out and meet the folks of Rebel. This is your home now." She stood and picked up sleeping PJ and placed her on a blanket on the colorful area rug Daisy had purchased for the room.

Daisy nodded, knowing she was right but still hesitant about tonight's outing.

Her grandmother continued. "It's also important to build a support system. A church home and community friends you can call upon when you need help."

"I hear you, Gran." She heard her, but she wasn't biting. Asking for help meant depending on people and her experience said that people always let you down.

"You're a mother now, so you've got to think like one. No more hiding in the back pew of church. You've got to get to know folks for the kiddos' sakes."

Daisy's chin came up at her grandmother's well-targeted words. "How do you know I was a back-pew lurker?"

Alice laughed and blew a short raspberry. "Please," she said with an exaggerated drawl. "I know my grand-daughter."

"I'm an introvert. There's nothing wrong with that."

Her grandmother stepped closer and lowered her voice. "There's a big difference between being an introvert and hiding from life. Since your daddy died, you've avoided engaging in anything that could leave you open to the pain of loss again." She shook her head. "I daresay, fifteen years later and losing your sister has only made things worse."

Daisy scrambled for a response, but her grandmother kept talking.

"And not to speak ill of the ex, but sweetheart, you can do better than a man who takes off the first time you need him."

"Gran!" Though she protested, Daisy knew the words were true.

"Go," her grandmother continued with a wave of a hand. "Allow yourself to have fun, and stop worrying about tomorrow. You're here because the good Lord led you here. Relax in that knowledge." She grinned and offered a mischievous wink. "Who knows, maybe you'll meet a nice cowboy."

Right. A nice cowboy who isn't terrified of my ready-made family.

Daisy mulled over the conversation with her grandmother as she guided the minivan to the outskirts of town and the turnoff to Rebel Ranch. Dating wasn't an option anymore. The kids required all her attention, and she wasn't going to allow them to get close to someone who had one foot out the door.

When she turned into the ranch drive and passed the iron arch, a young cowboy directing traffic pointed her to a parking area on the gravel. She parked and pulled down the visor to check her appearance one last time before she got out of the van.

Hundreds of tiny twinkle lights had been strung along the path to the ranch, and were laced through the overhead trees to create a starlit canopy. Though it wouldn't be completely dark for another hour and a half, the lights were still visible, shimmering among the foliage and providing a festive atmosphere. Tonight there was a slight breeze, bringing with it the now familiar scents of hay and horses and, yes, even manure. The closer Daisy got to the ranch, the stronger the pungent and tantalizing smells of roasting meat became, and her stomach rumbled in anticipation.

At the entrance to the event, an amply built middle-aged woman, whose pink cowboy hat sat perched on silver sky-high hair, greeted Daisy, handing her a stick-on name tag along with a black marker.

"Are you visiting Rebel, dear?" she asked.

"No. I live here now." Daisy wrote her name on the badge and handed back the marker before she peeled off the paper and placed the name tag on her new shirt. "I'm Daisy Anderson from the Rebel Police Department."

The woman grinned. "Welcome to town, Daisy Anderson. I'm Saylor Tuttle, the pastor's wife."

Daisy took the offered hand, warming at the enthusiastic greeting.

"I hope we'll see you in church on Sunday, dear."

"Yes. Of course. I'll be there."

"Wonderful. Now head on over to that first tent. We have beverages, and tables lined with side dishes and desserts. I hope you brought your appetite."

"I definitely did." She paused. "What's in the second tent?"

"There's a local country band warming up in there, and a portable dance floor has been put down. With the lake so close by, and this being the month of June, we try to keep the nightly moth, June bug and mosquito attacks to a minimum. The tents help, plus Reece had the grounds sprayed."

"I had no idea."

"Oh, yes. Keep your windows closed at night unless you have screens."

"Thank you for that information."

Daisy moved hesitantly toward the tents where groups of people stood around talking, laughing and eating. Amber flames danced in the firepit as a few folks sat on log benches chatting. Across the yard, to her right, she spotted Roscoe in jeans, a Western shirt and an oversize brass trophy buckle, chatting with a group of old-timers. When he raised his head and his gaze met hers, her partner offered a tip of his white hat and a thumbs-up with his bandaged appendage.

She couldn't help but smile in return.

To Daisy's left, Henna stood conversing with the tall, slim man she'd met earlier in the office.

Relieved to see familiar faces, the tension holding her shoulders rigid relaxed. A moment later her senses went on alert as Mitch stepped up to the firepit. He added several pieces of wood to the fire, causing the flames to shoot up and toss small bits of ruby embers and black ash into the air. When he stood and dusted off his hands, his gaze connected with hers. Surprise skittered across his face, and he offered a nod of greeting and the shadow of a smile.

Her heart fluttered and she rebuked the response. She was a practical woman, and practical women's hearts did not flutter.

As Mitch crossed the short distance between them, Daisy couldn't help but notice the subtle change that civilian clothes made. His take-no-prisoners stance seemed to have relaxed now that he was out of uniform. In a plaid Western shirt and faded jeans with boots and a black hat, he seemed like any other cowboy at the event. Except he wasn't. He was Mitch.

And even in civilian attire, the man was formidable. Suddenly it occurred to Daisy that Roscoe was right. Accusing her brand-new boss of coddling her probably wasn't the best of moves her first week on the job. She'd let it go. For now.

"Hey, you made it," he said.

"I said I'd be here."

"Yeah, you did." Mitch pushed his hat back and assessed her outfit. "Nice boots."

Had she imagined the twitching of his lips at the comment? "Um, thanks," Daisy said.

"Reece is busy. Let me get you acquainted with our community."

Mitch proceeded to introduce her to friendly locals who were eager to meet the town's newest law-enforcement officer. Daisy smiled and nodded, as Mitch chatted up the townsfolk and ranch guests like they were old friends. The police chief was much more of a people person than she would have guessed.

By the time they finished making the rounds nearly an hour later, Daisy's jaw ached from smiling. "That was my official trial by fire, right?" she asked.

He nodded. "Now you can say that you have been officially introduced to the town of Rebel," Mitch said.

"Oh, I believe that. I'll never remember everyone's name."

"A little overwhelming, huh?"

"Yes."

"They mean well, and they're sincere." His phone buzzed, and he pulled it from his pocket. "Reece needs my help. I trust you'll be all right on your own?"

"I keep reminding you that I'm a law-enforcement officer. I can handle crowd control."

"I'm referring to the curious folks who are going to want to chat it up with the new cop in town who looks like a Sheplers magazine advertisement."

"I, um… Sheplers?" Daisy stuttered, her tongue stuck to the roof of her mouth as Mitch walked away.

Look at you, friend.

Daisy turned to find Henna at her side, grinning.

"I hope you're aware that you've had Mitch Rainbolt's attention for the last sixty minutes," she said. "Folks are starting to talk."

"Folks?" Daisy cocked her head.

"The local gossips and pretty much every single woman in this town." Henna's eyes sparkled with amusement.

"He was just introducing me around."

Henna laughed. "No worries. They're simply bitterly jealous."

"Jealous? Of what?"

"That you snagged Mitch's attention for so long."

"But I told you—"

Henna raised a hand. "Tell that to his fan club. Daisy, the Rainbolt brothers are the most eligible bachelors Rebel has to offer. Mitch maybe more so because he couldn't care less."

Once again, Daisy glanced over at Mitch. He stood silhouetted against the fading sunset, tall with those broad shoulders and angular face. She shivered and turned away, her glance moving to Will Needleman.

"What about him?" Daisy asked.

Her friend's smile became tender as she looked across the grass at her companion. "Will? Oh, he's taken. I'm just not ready for him to know that. The truth is, the Rainbolts are far too complicated for me. I like a simple man."

Daisy choked on a laugh. "Did you just call Will simple?"

"Poor word choice." Henna smiled. "I prefer an uncomplicated, easygoing man. Will is that."

"Nice save."

"Thank you."

"Um, Henna?"

"Hmm?"

"What's Sheplers?" Daisy asked.

"A huge Western-wear store. They have one in Tulsa. Why?"

"Just curious."

Henna nodded. "Okay, now let's get down to important stuff. Have you eaten?"

"No, but I think I'm going to save the barbecue for later. I want dessert first."

"I respect that. I'm a meat and potatoes girl." Henna put a hand on her hip. "These curves don't happen by themselves, you know." She gestured toward the smoking grills. "I'll grab a hamburger and catch up with you later."

Daisy nodded and moved to the food tent. Her breath caught, and she clasped her hands together. An entire table was dedicated to pies. The tins sat side by side, each special in its own way. The apple was decorated with a golden brown lattice, the lemon meringue piled high with a perfectly whipped peak of lightly toasted meringue. She put her hands in her back pockets to fight the strong urge to break off a piece of crust to sample the browned goodness of her favorite—pecan, whose glossy caramel and nut filling glowed beneath the soft tent lights.

Instead, she stood for minutes eyeing the varieties. Without hesitation, Daisy took less than a sliver of each. Satisfied with the arrangement on her plate, she found a seat by the firepit and began to evaluate her selection before digging in.

"How's that pie?" a familiar masculine voice asked as she chased the last crumb of pecan around her plate with her finger.

"Which one?" Daisy licked a bit of apple pie from her fork and savored the flavors before looking up at Mitch.

He blinked. "Ah… How many did you taste?"

"I've tried them all and found none wanting. Except the opportunity for a second helping." She scooped up the last dab of meringue on the plate and swirled the light confection on her tongue. This was near to perfection. Tonight, she was sitting at the feet of a master, and Daisy knew she must find out who the master was.

"I left you near the barbecue. Did you have dinner?"

"All in good time." She tapped her plate with the side of her fork. "Is there a bakery in town?"

"No. Just the donut place and the Piggly Wiggly. The diner will sell you a whole pie if you catch them early in the day."

"No bakery?"

"You have to go to Cleveland or Hominy if you want a proper bakery."

"Then who makes these pies?"

"Luna."

"Luna." Daisy looked up at him again. "May I meet this Luna?"

"Yeah, sure. She's up at the mess hall. The big kitchen is there."

"How do we get there?" she asked.

His eyes rounded. "You want to go now?"

Daisy glanced down at her empty paper plate. "Yes, please."

Mitch pointed to the trash barrel and recycle bin, where she disposed of her plate and plastic fork. He led her from the firepit to the walking path that went from the big guesthouse into the woods.

"Careful. The sun is setting, and it can be dark on the path with all this foliage. There are pole lights at intervals, but you never know what you might run into."

Daisy pointed to her boots. "I'm prepared this time."

"I noticed that." An amused smile touched his lips. "So, what's with your pie obsession?" he asked.

"Some girls dream of being a dancer, a doctor, a teacher. I've always dreamed of baking full-time. Pies are my specialty."

"So why didn't you become a baker?"

"That's something I'm still trying to figure out." She concentrated on the dirt path, her eyes on the toes of her new boots.

"How did a baker become a cop?"

"Oh, you know. The usual reasons one goes into law enforcement." She stepped around a rock, and matched her strides to Mitch's long ones.

He turned and looked at her. "Are there usual reasons?"

"Absolutely. For me it was because my father was in law enforcement," she said. "You know how that goes. Young kid, idolizes their father."

"No, but I'll take your word for it. Is your father still active?"

"I, um… We lost him when I was a kid." Daisy scrambled to segue the conversation away from herself. "What about you? Why don't you work here at the ranch like your brother?"

"When we took over the ranch, the operation wasn't bringing in enough income to sustain both Reece and me. The place was rented out and had been maintained over the years, but there weren't cattle or horses. It was just the land."

"Why Reece? Not you? You're the oldest."

Mitch raised his brows at her question. "My brother is the visionary when it comes to the ranch."

"And you? The usual reasons to go into law enforcement, right?" She stuck her hands in her front pockets as they walked.

"Explain what you mean by that," he said.

"The usual reasons? Family legacy, or control. Maybe altruism."

"I guess you think you've figured me out?"

She looked him up and down. Did she dare answer? "Offhand, I'd say control is your driving motivation. The land, animals and Mother Nature are defiant. But the law, the law is all about rules. There is very little gray."

"Here I thought I became a cop because I wanted to make a difference in the lives of people around me. Specifically my siblings, who needed a paycheck and medical insurance." His expression was unreadable as he met her gaze. "Instead, you're telling me it's all about my control issues."

Daisy swallowed and attempted to backpedal. Once again, she'd put her foot in her mouth by being honest. "I apologize, Chief. And you're right. I don't know you well enough to know your issues." She paused, horrified that she had dug herself deeper. "I mean *if* you have issues."

"We can agree to disagree on that one," he said. "I don't have issues."

"Again, I apologize."

"Not to worry. It's possible that maybe I am touchy about the subject."

Mitch offered a glimmer of a smile, enough for Daisy to release the breath she'd been holding.

"I only said maybe," he murmured.

As he said the words, a blur of an animal raced across the path and Daisy nearly stumbled. Mitch grabbed her arm before she fell.

"Thanks." She stepped back from his touch and glanced around. "What was that?"

"If I had to guess, I'd say it was a roadrunner."

"A real roadrunner."

"Yep, a real roadrunner." He led her around to the front of the building and pulled open the huge glass doors of the ranch mess hall. "This way."

Daisy followed him to the granite serving counter that ran in a horseshoe shape, separating the tables from the main kitchen. "Look at this place," she murmured while gazing through the open doors into the spacious kitchen.

"Just in time, Señor Mitch." A petite woman with a riot of black curls threaded with gray and pulled back with a turquoise comb came bustling from the back to greet them. Adjusting her pristine white-buttoned chef's coat, she grinned, the smile lighting up her round face. "I have more desserts to take to the party. You get the golf cart. *Sí?*"

"Yes, ma'am." He looked to Daisy. "Luna Diaz, this is Daisy Anderson."

"Go get the golf cart," Luna said with a commanding flip of her hand. "I will take care of your friend."

Mitch looked from Daisy to the petite chef. "I'll be right back."

The older woman grinned and stepped forward to take Daisy's hands. "So, Mitch finally has a special friend. It's about time."

"Oh, no," Daisy said, alarmed at the inference. "I'm a

police officer. Mitch is my boss." Daisy cleared her throat. "I wanted to meet you. I'm an aspiring pâtissière. Self-taught. I'm not a professional like you."

"We are kindred spirits then. You and I will schedule a time to chat after the party."

"That would be very nice, thank you."

"I must go make a phone call." Luna smiled, her eyes bright with amusement, as though she knew a secret. "But you may look around. Open the cupboards. Have fun."

"Thank you." Daisy held back the bubble of excitement at the opportunity to wander through the professional kitchen. She ran a hand over the stainless-steel counters and stopped to examine the big convection oven and the commercial mixer. At the sight of the reversible dough sheeter, she paused and sighed, unable to contain a smile. Oh, to have access to this equipment.

She turned when the big glass doors opened and Henna and Will entered the kitchen.

"Hey, Daisy. They sent us for more desserts," Henna said. While she was all smiles, Will fidgeted and looked away.

"We're going to take them. Mitch has gone for the golf cart," Daisy said.

"Great. We better get going." Henna slipped her arm through Will's and pulled him toward the door.

As Daisy circled the counter, her gaze caught on a red swatch of cotton on the ground. *Henna's*. She stepped outside, hoping to return the bandanna. In the darkness, the couple's conversation drifted to her.

"Mitch will tell Daisy on Monday," Henna said.

"Uh-oh. Remind me to stay out of Rebel next week," Will returned.

"This is all your fault, Will."

"Henna," Will protested.

Daisy froze, unable to move. The voices faded as the twosome walked farther down the path.

"Daisy?"

She turned to find Mitch behind her.

"Everything okay?"

She stepped back into the kitchen, letting the screen door slowly close behind her. "What were they talking about?"

"Who?"

"Will and Henna." Daisy met Mitch's gaze and searched his face. "Henna said you were going to tell me something on Monday?"

Mitch grimaced and rubbed a hand over his jaw, but he didn't look away. "We've had a glitch in our funding."

Daisy's pulse tapped a staccato beat of panic. *A glitch?* She knew all about glitches. "A last man in is the first man out glitch?"

"Sort of."

"Sort of?" she choked out.

"I've got the golf cart outside. Let's load up the food, and then we can talk."

They worked in silence for moments. Daisy sneaked peeks at Mitch as she worked, hoping to figure out just how bad the situation really was. Had she lost a job she'd barely begun? As usual, his face remained a mask.

"Gracias," Luna said as they grabbed two flats of cookies and a tray of pies. She handed Daisy her card. "Call me and we will have coffee."

Daisy nodded numbly.

"Are you all right?" Luna asked, peering closely.

"Yes," Daisy murmured. "It's all good."

"Call me," Luna repeated. She patted Daisy's arm before she went back into the kitchen.

Mitch got in the golf cart and started the engine. "I'd planned to talk to you on Monday."

"That much I understood." Daisy nodded. "You knew something this afternoon and blew me off." Frustration simmered inside her, and she struggled to maintain a calm she wasn't feeling. "I'm out of a job, and you didn't say a thing."

"You aren't out of a job." Again, Mitch's gaze was steady as his dark eyes met hers.

"Sounds like it to me."

"Are you going to get in?" he asked, gesturing toward the passenger seat.

Daisy opened her mouth and then closed it. She didn't even know how to address him. Mitch? Chief? Was he still her boss? "I'd like to walk."

"I can't leave you like this."

"Leave me how? Humiliated? Shocked? Pick one." She crossed her arms. "I don't think you understand. I just met half the town. Not only am I embarrassed, but I'm unemployed. Unemployed with a mortgage and five kids."

He slowly got out of the golf cart and faced her, his gaze resolute. "I won't allow that to happen. This is my fault and I'm going to fix it."

"How?"

"I don't know how yet. But we have until the end of the summer to prove to the county that the Rebel Police Department deserves the funding we need to maintain your position."

"Prove? How?"

"Civic engagement. The new buzzword. That's how we're going to keep our budget from tanking."

"Civic engagement," Daisy murmured while kicking at the dirt with the toe of her boot. She was silent, collecting herself before she lifted her head and met his gaze. "You should have told me today."

"You're right. I apologize. My only defense is that I didn't want to spoil the evening for you."

"It's not your job to take care of me. I've been doing that for a very long time."

"Maybe so." He offered a slow nod and released a long breath. "You have every right to be angry."

"I don't know what I am."

"And you don't want a ride?"

"No, thank you."

Without another word, Mitch got back into the golf cart and turned it around.

Daisy kept her eyes on the vehicle until she could no longer see the ruby taillights. Then she gave the hard red dirt a swift kick.

How had everything gone from hopeful anticipation to disaster?

She began to walk. Ahead of her, through the trees, the sun said good-night to the day as the stars sprinkled across the sky began to shine. Daisy kept walking, even as the weight of what happened pressed down. She had five children depending on her. The move to Rebel had been prayerful, with the deep awareness that she and the kids needed what the town could offer. A life without the rug being pulled out from under them...again.

Everything would be okay, she reassured herself. Somehow, she'd find her way to the other side of this mess. She had to.

Chapter Four

When Mitch's cell rang he debated the merits of ignoring the interruption. He hadn't had a day off in weeks. Not that he was exactly relaxing. Hard work was the best way to cure what ailed you, his grandfather always said. Right now, Daisy Anderson was what ailed him.

He wiped his brow with his forearm and took a peek at the sun, beating down from the cloudless blue sky. With a grunt of resignation, he pulled off his work gloves before reaching for the ringing cell phone in his back pocket. He recognized the number as his younger brother's.

"You need something, Tuck?" Mitch asked.

"Hi, to you too," his brother returned. "What are you doing?"

"Yard work." His gaze skipped over the fenced yard that separated his property from his neighbors'.

"About done?" Tucker asked.

"Why?" Fighting a yawn, Mitch glanced at his watch. Three p.m. He'd been up since dawn, after giving in to a losing battle with insomnia. The clock moved slowly when you were paying penance. Every time he closed his eyes, he saw the painful expression on Daisy's face last night at Rebel Ranch, and it was eating him up that he'd put it there.

"Because I need a favor."

"First Reece, and now you. And by the way, why weren't you at the ranch shindig?"

"Life conspired against me."

"What's going on?"

"Absolutely swamped at the clinic. Besides a few minor emergencies, it's spring and we're overrun with kittens. I'm desperate for foster homes."

He grabbed his water bottle and took a long swig before answering. "Tuck, I took two kittens off your hands just last week."

"I appreciate that, but they're coming in faster than they're going out the door. I exhausted most of my usual foster homes in April and May."

"I don't do kittens."

"This is a cat, Mitch."

"I don't have time to handle a special needs cat."

"What makes you think it's special needs?"

"Because I know you."

Tucker released a frustrated breath. "She's blind, but she doesn't need special care. All she needs is a chance and some love."

Silence stretched as Mitch studied the red dirt caked on his old boots. Twenty years since their mother passed and their absentee father took off, and Mitch still couldn't say no to his siblings.

"You still there?" Tucker asked.

"Yeah, still here and still trying to figure out how to move and not leave a forwarding address."

His brother laughed. "You talk a good story, but I know better. You'd hate it without your annoying family around."

Mitch offered a noncommittal grunt. His brother was right, but no point in letting him know that.

"So, what do you say?"

"What's the story with this one?"

"Only a year old. Returned to the clinic because the owner's fiancé is highly allergic."

Mitch searched for a protest but could only mutter a weak, "I don't know."

"I wouldn't ask if I wasn't desperate," Tucker returned.

"Will this cat be okay alone when I'm at work?"

"Sure. Set her up in the guestroom with the door closed. Let her get used to the new situation before you give her free rein."

"What about Mutt?" He turned to check on his aged hound, snoring beneath the lazy limbs of a willow tree.

Tucker laughed again. This time long and hard. "Mutt? He sleeps through tornados. A cat won't bother him."

"So says the guy who told me Mutt was a foster. Here temporarily until you could rehome him. I believe that was five years ago."

"Everything turned out all right, didn't it? You love that dog."

"You're missing the point."

"Mitch, come on. Can you help me out?"

"Yeah, I guess so." He blew out a puff of air. "But this is the last time."

"Last time. Got it." Tucker cleared his throat. "Ahh… Could you come here to get her? The twins are fussy and their nanny is out of town."

"The girls are at the clinic with you?"

"Yeah. Been here all day."

"Why are they fussy?"

"They're two-year-olds."

"No. I'm serious."

"So am I. You ask me questions as though I know what I'm doing. I haven't got a clue. I'm a single Dad, remember?"

Mitch's chest tightened at the words. Single father. Widower. Tuck was one of the good guys. He didn't deserve the knocks life had given him.

"Give me a chance to get cleaned up and put away the lawn mower."

"Great. Come by the house. We're leaving the clinic shortly." The relief in his brother's voice nearly did Mitch in.

"Tell you what," Mitch said. "Why don't I bring dinner with me?"

"You don't have to do that."

"I could use a night off from my own cooking."

"Thanks, bro. That would be great." Tucker paused. "I don't care what Reece says about you being a cranky old man. You're okay in my book."

Mitch gave a sarcastic chuckle. "Funny, kid. Real funny."

Twenty minutes later Mitch pulled his truck into a spot in front of the Arrowhead Diner. He couldn't help but notice Daisy's minivan with the oversize flower sticker on the rear bumper, parked at the end of the row of cars directly in front of Rebel Reads Bookstore and the Tallgrass Inn.

She was probably at the bookstore on a Saturday afternoon. Rebel was a busy town this time of year. No reason to think their paths would cross today. He'd make things right on Monday.

A waitress with a bright smile and an effusive hello greeted him when he pushed open the glass door.

"What can I do for you, Chief Rainbolt?"

Mitch placed his order and offered his credit card.

"That'll be about ten, fifteen minutes. Have a seat and I'll bring you a cup of coffee. Fresh pot will be ready in a jiffy."

"Thank you, Ruth."

He scanned the room, surprised when his gaze landed on a familiar redhead seated at a table in the corner, her back to him.

Daisy.

He glanced at the door, calculating his next move before muttering under his breath, "Time to man up."

As if sensing his presence, she turned. When their eyes connected, he saw the pain in hers. And something else.

An expression that said he was the last person she wanted to see.

Things were about to get uncomfortable real quick.

As he got closer to her table, he could tell that she hadn't slept much either. The normally bright blue eyes were somber and dull with dark shadows beneath them. Her strawberry-blond hair remained in the plait she'd worn last night.

"Officer Anderson," he said.

"I'm off duty," she said. "Surely you can call me Daisy."

"Mind if I sit down? *Daisy?*"

She waved a hand toward the chair across the table from her.

"You still angry with me?" he asked.

"Angry?" Daisy mused, her hands cupping a near-empty mug. "I don't do angry. I learned a long time ago that there is little satisfaction or value in anger."

"I disagree. There's nothing wrong with a good bout of mad before you move on."

She didn't answer, simply drained the contents of her mug.

"Where are the kids?"

"Home. Rough day. My grandmother kicked me out of the house."

Mitch blinked. "Excuse me?"

Her eyes jerked to him. "No. That is not what I meant. Rough morning with the kids. Sometimes they miss their parents so much it breaks my heart."

"I imagine so."

She stared at him. "Do you?"

"Yeah. You won't find anyone who gets what you're going through more than me."

"You have children, then?"

"Ah, no. I raised my brothers and sisters. All in all, there were five Rainbolt kids under one roof, and that roof was pretty shaky."

Before he realized what he was doing, Mitch pulled out his wallet and slid a weathered photo across the table. The urge to let Daisy know she wasn't alone overrode his good sense. "All five of us. We lost Levi five years ago."

We? Mitch swallowed hard against the pain. He'd lost Levi. Plain and simple.

Daisy picked up the photograph and studied the image, her brows scrunched up as if in pain. "I'm so sorry."

Mitch nodded at the words. "All I'm trying to say is I do get what you're going through."

He sensed it the minute her guard dropped, and the tension eased from her shoulders. The concern in her eyes was nearly his undoing. For the first time in a long time, maybe in forever, he nearly gave in to the urge to talk about his road to today.

As quickly as the thought came, he checked himself. This was about Daisy.

"What's going on with the kids?" he asked.

"Missing their parents." Her finger traced a circle in the condensation on her water glass as she spoke. "Grief is a funny thing. You go for days without stumbling and then, out of the blue, a little thing can trigger the pain." She took a ragged breath. "My grandmother suggested I go into town and take a break," Daisy murmured. With one last look at the photograph, she handed it back to him.

"Smart grandmother."

"Yes."

The smiling waitress interrupted them with a mug dangling from her fingers and a fresh pot of coffee. Daisy nodded when she offered to fill her cup.

"Cream with that. Right, Chief Rainbolt?"

"Yeah. Right. Thank you."

"My pleasure." She set a small pitcher of cream on the table along with the coffee carafe. "I noticed you liked those chocolate muffins when you were here last time, so I had the cook put some on your order. No charge."

"Uh, thank you."

She offered Daisy a quick nod of her chin. "Your order will be right up, ma'am."

"Thank you." Daisy turned to him as the waitress walked away. "You have a fan."

"Purely demographics. The population of this town is skewed heavily in favor of single, widowed and divorced women. Sometimes it gets downright awkward."

"You don't date?"

"Have you had a chance to check out Rebel Reads?" he asked. "They have a children's reading hour once a week."

Daisy laughed at his obvious attempt to change the subject. The effect immediately lightened the mood between them. "No," she said. "I haven't. It's on my list."

Mitch poured cream into his mug, stirred the coffee and then placed the spoon on his napkin, while he carefully weighing his next words. Daisy probably wouldn't appreciate his free advice. However, that had never stopped him before. "Thought about vacation Bible school? Faith can get them through times like this."

"I agree." Her eyes rounded. "You're absolutely right. Faith is what's gotten me through."

With his gaze fixed on Daisy, Mitch silently echoed the sentiment. "Might do them some good to be around other kids too," he continued. "It's only a week. Not like it's a long-term commitment."

"Isn't it too late enroll?"

"Nope. Sign up at church tomorrow. It starts on Monday."

"I'll do that. Thank you."

"And don't forget about Luna."

"Luna?"

"Yeah, she tracked me down during the event cleanup

last night and let me know how much she was looking forward to meeting with you."

Daisy's jaw sagged slightly. "How do you have time to run the world while you're policing Rebel?"

Mitch paused at the words and then chuckled. "I'm very, very organized."

An easy silence settled between them before Daisy looked up and met his gaze. "I've been thinking about what you said."

Mitch scrambled to figure out what she was talking about. "What I said?"

"Civic engagement."

"We'll brainstorm Monday at the staff meeting. I'm sure we'll come up with something. No sense you worrying about that today."

"I've had a few ideas," she said, her expression hesitant.

"You have?"

"Do you mind if I run them by you?"

"Ah, sure."

"Have you thought about self-defense classes taught by the Rebel Police Department?"

"Self-defense classes. In Rebel?" He rubbed his jaw. "Never fly."

"Seriously? You're shutting down my suggestion like that?"

Mitch paused, searching for a way to explain country life to the city girl. "This is a rural community. Most folks don't lock their doors. I'm not sure they'd see a need for a self-defense class."

"Then we don't call it self-defense. We'll pitch it as personal safety."

He narrowed his gaze. "Who would teach this class?"

"Me."

"You? What are your qualifications?"

Daisy took a sip of coffee before she answered. "I've

taught women safety and self-defense on college campuses across the Denver area. Actually, I've launched several programs."

He blinked. "You didn't mention that on your résumé."

"I didn't want to appear overqualified. The truth is, I could have had my pick of any urban police department. There were very few small-town positions open."

"That's because no one ever leaves."

"Exactly and I don't blame them." She gestured with a hand. "I want to fit in here and stay awhile, as well. I'm not here to usher in change. We both have a problem, and I think I can help."

Mitch pondered the feasibility of her idea for a moment. It just might work. "There's no money in the budget for overtime."

"I'm not asking for overtime. I thought that if I'm targeting civic engagement, maybe you'll let someone else babysit Roscoe."

His head jerked up at the comment. "You're not babysitting Roscoe. Where did you get that idea?"

"My esteemed partner may have mentioned that you have us both on light duty."

Mitch clamped his jaw tight for a moment, reining in his irritation. Roscoe was going to be a thorn in his posterior until the day he retired. "Don't believe everything Officer McFarland spouts. Whatever decisions I make are in the best interest of our team."

"Fair enough, and what about my idea?" Daisy continued.

"You can give it a shot, and I'm willing to divert some of your patrol hours to this project."

"Does that mean you think it will work?"

"It means that I'm willing to give it a shot, and yeah—" he paused "—it could work."

"I'll get right on it, then. Thanks, Chief."

"Maybe you could call me Mitch when we aren't on duty."

The corners of her mouth twitched, and her eyes shimmered with amusement. "Mitch."

He found himself mesmerized by the sound of his name on her lips.

Mitch cleared his throat and focused his attention on the coffee carafe. "And your other ideas?" he finally asked.

"Maybe I'll hold on to those until I can present them at the staff meeting."

"You think I'm going to shut you down again."

"Or maybe I'm not convinced you have as much at stake in this situation as I do."

"I'd take offense at that except you're right. Rebel desperately needs that funding, but there is no denying that you've got much more on the line."

"There's one more thing," Daisy murmured.

"Go ahead."

"I'm going to give this initiative two hundred percent. If we succeed, and I plan on it, I'd like my own vehicle at the end of training. My own vehicle and no partner."

"You've only been here a week. Training is usually five to eight weeks."

"Five to eight weeks." Daisy blew a raspberry and shook her head. "If I was straight out of the academy, I'd understand that. Don't you think you can shorten it?"

Mitch assessed the resolute expression in her eyes, and the determined set of her chin as she boldly stared him down. "What I think," he said, "is that you're a lot more tenacious than I anticipated."

"Is that a nice word for stubborn?" The response was accompanied by a chuckle. "Either way, you can thank my father for that."

"I'll agree to revisit this once we get the civic engagement plans in motion," Mitch said.

She met his gaze. "I'm not giving up until I'm in my own vehicle and we've won that funding."

"Music to my ears," he said.

When their waitress appeared again, she slid Daisy's entrée in front of her and placed a box that held two take-out bags in front of Mitch.

Daisy assessed his order. "I guess you're hungry."

"I'm taking this to Tucker's. It's been a tough day for everyone. He's a single father on his last thread."

She cocked her head and her expression softened. "You're a nice person, Mitch."

"Let's not get carried away." He stood. "Maybe I'll see you and your family in church tomorrow. Otherwise, I'll see you on Monday."

"Thanks," she murmured.

"For what?"

"For listening."

"Anytime, Daisy."

Once he was in the truck, Mitch placed the take-out bag on the seat next to him. For a moment, he played back his conversation with Daisy.

The woman didn't back down. He'd give her that. Spunk and determination were part of the package. Daisy Anderson was definitely the complete package, tied up with a huge heart.

There was no denying how much he admired and respected her.

He liked her too. And he hadn't made that admission about any woman in a very long time.

Sliding the wallet from his pocket, Mitch took out the photograph once more. He leaned against the seat and stared straight ahead out the windshield, as his thumb made a slow pass over the lines of faded memories and he reminded himself why he couldn't risk any more heartache in his life.

* * *

"Safety education classes," Daisy repeated.

"That's what I thought you said." Roscoe carefully inspected the Monday donuts Henna brought in before he settled on a glazed maple bar. When he turned to Daisy, his face was screwed up with displeasure.

"Isn't it a great idea?" Henna asked as she sorted through the weekend mail.

"Can't say you took the words out of my mouth on that one." He stared into the depths of his coffee cup and frowned. "What happened to the Rebel Roast? I can't drink this sludge."

"You're drinking it faster than our budget can keep up," Henna said.

Daisy resisted the urge to stick her tongue out at the cranky senior officer. Roscoe had definitely poured himself a heaping bowl of his brand of negative before he showed up to work. That meant another interesting eight hours on patrol. She headed to the coffeepot for a fill-up while praying under her breath for patience.

"I don't understand how the county can renege on a promise," he groused. "Sounds unconstitutional to me."

"It is what it is. Your attitude isn't helping," Henna said. She looked him straight in the eye. "If we want to keep Daisy's position and ensure a cost-of-living raise, we've got to come up with an idea that's better than anyone else's."

"How do you propose to do that?" Roscoe asked. "The last good idea that came out of this office was twenty years ago when they got rid of white Stetsons with the duty uniform."

"I heard that, McFarland," Mitch called from his office.

"Am I right?" Roscoe shot back.

"I like to think that a few good ideas have emerged in the last four years," Mitch said. He stepped into the staff area of the department with a coffee cup in hand.

Daisy's back was to Mitch, and she kept it that way. She wasn't certain how she felt after their conversation on Saturday. She'd been in a male dominated job for over nine years, and it never presented a problem before. So why did her pulse quicken in his presence? Why now? And why this man? He was her boss, and she needed to remember that.

"I do have some good news," Henna said in a singsong voice. Her dark eyes sparkled as she faced her coworkers.

Henna was most definitely on the far end of the optimism spectrum. She was a contrast to Roscoe the pessimist and Mitch the cynic. The woman managed to transform the atmosphere everywhere she went into something bright and shining.

"I'll take good news," Mitch said.

"Pastor Tuttle has offered to let us use the church activity room free of charge for the safety education classes." She offered a mischievous grin. "And there's more."

"Uh-oh," Roscoe muttered. "Maybe I ought to sit down."

"Drumroll, please. So far, we have fifty sign-ups. Can you believe it?"

"Fifty?" Daisy asked. Her idea was a success.

"That's right," Henna returned.

"We haven't even made it official," Mitch said.

"Daisy and I discussed it on Sunday before church. I thought she said that you liked the idea." She glanced between Daisy and Mitch. "Was I wrong?"

"No. I guess not," Mitch said almost hesitantly.

Henna picked up a glazed donut. "The Henna train is coming through. Get on board or get run over."

Daisy hid a grin behind her coffee mug. She was right. Daisy might have talked a good one to Mitch on Saturday, but clearly Henna was conducting this train.

"Why are there so many sign-ups?" Mitch asked, looking genuinely perplexed.

"Safety education is a hot topic," Daisy said.

"Or maybe our police chief is," Henna murmured.

Mitch's eyes rounded. "You didn't put my name out there, did you?"

"Of course not." Henna smiled. "I said that you and Daisy are teaching the class."

Daisy winced. Uh-oh.

"No, way," Mitch returned.

"All you have to do is stand at the back of the class and nod. A small price to pay to save our budget and Daisy's job."

"How many of those eager sign-ups are of the female persuasion?" Roscoe asked.

"All of them."

Roscoe burst out laughing, nearly spilling his coffee.

"Nope. No way," Mitch said.

"Chief, you know every woman in a fifty-mile radius will sign up if your name is attached to the project."

Roscoe continued to laugh. "Sounds like they already did."

While Mitch's attention was focused on Henna, Daisy allowed herself to assess her boss. Her gaze skimmed over the broad shoulders and handsome profile. He was definitely the complete package.

Henna's plan was solid, though the idea of teaching a room filled with love-struck women was oddly annoying.

"Ignore Roscoe," Henna said.

"No problem," Daisy said. "I get that the chief is the draw."

Mitch crossed his arms and pinned his gaze on Henna. "So that's your plan. You want me to just stand at the back of the class?"

Henna shrugged. "Unless you have a better idea."

"I'd be happy to review my curriculum with you," Daisy said. "I mean if you'd like to teach."

His gaze met Daisy's, and then he nodded in dismissal. "Sure. Fine. We can discuss this later."

Daisy swallowed. Mitch was definitely not fine.

"Anything else?" he asked, obviously eager to move along.

"Daisy and I took the kids on a road trip after church yesterday," Henna added. "We drove through a few of the towns in the area and picked up the local newspapers." She pulled a stack of weeklies from a tote on her desk. "There are a lot of good things going on in the county."

"And…" Mitch prompted.

"One word," Henna said. "Ride-along."

He raised his mug as if in toast. "I'm all for great ideas. Ride-alongs are not one of them."

"Chief, you can't veto everything." Henna offered a loud scoffing sound. "A ride-along would foster good community relations. Everyone is doing it."

"First, sure I can. That's why my name is on that door. And second, ride-alongs are absolutely something to look into. For the future. The liability issue alone is going to take some time to work through."

Daisy nodded. She had to admit he was right about the legal aspect.

Mitch rubbed his chin in that way that was becoming familiar to Daisy as code for him carefully considering his words.

"This department should have stepped up our game a long time ago. I take responsibility for that. Now it's the eleventh hour for Rebel. We need to do something bigger and better than the competition. Make no mistake, every small town in this county is vying for those funds. It will take a remarkable plan to secure the pot for us."

"You're right, Chief," Henna said. "We have to do something that will stand out when our paperwork is turned in."

"Exactly," Mitch said. "Think long-term benefit and continued liaison between the police department and the community."

Daisy observed the exchange as ideas ping-ponged through her mind. Finally, unable to listen quietly, she cleared her throat. "I haven't been here long enough to be very knowledgeable about Rebel, however, it seems to me that we have to figure out what the citizens need."

"Need?" Roscoe echoed. He frowned as though she was speaking a foreign language.

"Yes. What's missing in this town? What project will also be a unifying factor that will bring everyone together?"

"That's easy," Henna said. "We need a place where everyone can meet. A town hall or community center for special events and meetings. Something that offers opportunities for every demographic of Rebel."

"Yes," Daisy murmured. Henna seemed to get what she was trying to say.

"That's pie in the sky because we don't have the time or the funds to build anything," Roscoe grumbled. "Didn't you hear the chief? We have less than three months."

"Repurpose." Henna snapped her fingers. "What about the old library building?"

When Mitch's face lit up, Daisy knew he was starting to get it.

"You're right," he said. "The building is just sitting there empty."

"Where is Rebel's library now?" Daisy asked.

"It expanded and is now part of the county system. They moved around the corner to Second Street about five years ago," Henna said.

"The former library building belongs to the city, and it's got some historical relevance we can play on. The old-timers in this town would love to see it being utilized again. All we'd have to do is raise money for utilities and cleanup. We can staff the place with volunteers," Mitch continued. "I think you have something here, Henna."

"Not me. This was definitely a collaborative effort," Henna returned with a nod toward Daisy.

"It'll give the kids a place to congregate after school and in the summer," Mitch mused.

"If the police department offered a few programs, even better," Daisy said.

"What kind of programs could we offer?" Roscoe asked.

"Oh, you know," Daisy said. "First aid, babysitting. That sort of thing."

"Maybe you've got something there, Daisy."

Daisy blinked at Roscoe's words of approval. When Mitch offered a thoughtful shake of his head, she realized that everyone was engaged with the idea. So maybe, just maybe, they were on their way to a solution.

"Lots of towns offer a junior police academy for teens and preteens," Daisy continued, buoyed by the interest. "They do cleanup and food drives and other community service activities. It has the added benefit of changing kids' perception of law enforcement, as well."

"Daisy, that's really a great idea," Henna said.

Mitch nodded. "I like it."

Her gaze spanned the room and the eager faces, encouraging her to continue.

"The thing about a community center is it serves all age groups," she began. "Women's groups, senior citizens, small business. We start by securing a building, and then this will be an ongoing initiative."

"The mayor will be on board," Mitch said. "Next year is an election year. We get it rolling, and he can take credit. All we have to do is get his approval to use the building and appoint a citizen committee to oversee the project."

"Will the local businesses step up?" Daisy asked.

"Eagle Donuts will," Henna said. "I'm certain the other business owners in town will follow suit. It's good for business. This will bring our rural community to town beyond tourist season."

"You're right, Henna. Just remember to delegate. We want to involve as many people in the community as possible," Mitch said.

"You got it, Chief. I can tell you that this is the most interesting challenge I've had on the job since I started here." Henna clapped her hands together. "I've always wanted to give back to Rebel in a way that will make a difference. This is just that opportunity."

"How do we raise the funds to get this off the ground?" Daisy asked. Though she was thrilled with everyone's response, she didn't dare get her hopes up until all the details were ironed out.

"Car wash?" Roscoe suggested.

"That can work," Henna said. "I'm sure the high school kids will get behind that."

"I'd love to organize a bake sale," Daisy said.

"Are you sure?" Henna asked. "You're already teaching classes."

"I'll take your lead and delegate," Daisy said. "I'm thinking Luna Diaz and my grandmother." That combination was a guarantee of success.

"I'll help with a bake sale," Roscoe said.

"Roscoe, that is so sweet of you," Henna said.

"Nah, don't be giving me too much credit. I follow the food."

"How can I get Rebel Ranch involved?" Mitch asked. "And when I say Rebel Ranch, I mean my brother."

"Would Reece consider an event at the ranch?" Henna asked.

"Sure," Mitch said. "Reece is the social butterfly in the family."

Daisy smiled at the remark. Having met his brother, she had to agree.

"You know, when the church needed a new roof, they held a fancy per plate party." Roscoe glanced at everyone. "I'm just saying."

"Dinner and dancing and Luna's food," Henna said.

When the department admin looked at Mitch, he held up his hands. "I said I'd ask Reece, but I'm not the person you want handling dinner and dancing."

"Fine. I'll coordinate with Reece."

"And I'll talk to the mayor," Mitch said. "Are we set?" he asked Henna.

"Yes. I'll work up a business plan to use the old library building and officially draw up everyone's assignments." She turned to Daisy. "That funding is ours."

Daisy wanted to believe her. Either way, she couldn't discount the fact that this was her second week on the job, and despite the looming budget issues she'd never felt so part of a community. She only prayed that today's brainstorming meeting hadn't lulled her into a false sense of hope. Despite Henna's encouraging words, there was no guarantee she'd be here at the end of summer.

Mitch turned and headed into his office. "I'll call the mayor's office now before the morning gets old."

The desk phone rang, and Henna reached for it. "Yes, ma'am. Thank you. We'll put out a BOLO immediately. Yes. ma'am. We'll keep you posted."

She hung up the phone and turned to the officers. "The cherub is missing. Summer has officially begun."

"Yeah, howdy," Roscoe said with a punch of his fist into the air. "How about we offer a reward this year? Maybe a dozen Eagle maple bars to the first officer to spot the cherub."

"I can do that," Henna said with a grin.

"What's going on?" Daisy asked. Just when she thought she was beginning to fit in, she realized that the department had a backstory she was clueless about.

"The cherub is missing from one of our senior citizens' front yard." Roscoe rinsed out his coffee cup and placed it on the counter.

Daisy blinked, searching both Henna's and Roscoe's face for the punchline. "The what?"

"Cherub," Roscoe said. "It's a statue of a chubby, naked—"

"I know what a cherub is. Why would someone steal a cherub statue?"

"This is summer in Rebel," Roscoe said. "The town is full of kids with nothing else to do but make my hair gray."

Daisy assessed his shiny scalp.

"That's a saying, missy."

"They stole a cherub." Daisy assessed her fellow officers once again. Sure, the crime stats in Rebel were much lower than in Denver, but this bordered on laughable. "You're kidding, right?"

"Not kidding. It's happened every single summer for as long as I can remember," Henna said. "The cherub going missing signifies the official start of summer."

Roscoe grabbed the keys to the patrol vehicle off the wall. "We take a report from the vic, and then we wait for the stolen property to show up."

Daisy downed her coffee and grabbed her ball cap. "You know it's going to show up? How?"

"Same story every year," Roscoe said.

"Another reason why we need a community center," Henna called after them. "The Rebel Police Department could use some good publicity instead of this cherub business that goes on every year."

"So we're going to spend the next eight hours looking for the statue?" Daisy followed him out the door to the patrol vehicle.

"Naw. That's a waste of time. It'll show up in a few day…or weeks. They like to torment us."

She opened the passenger door of the Crown Vic. "So you never find out who the culprit is?"

"Nope and I'm not expending any energy trying to figure it out, so don't get any ideas."

"Why not investigate? That is our job, Roscoe."

"Not worth the time. They'd only get off with a warning anyhow."

"You're telling me Mitch is okay with this?"

"Mitch's little brothers were the instigators that started this ten or so years ago. The whole thing puts him in a bad mood."

Daisy released a chuckle. "I get that it might be embarrassing, given Mitch's family history, but come on. A crime has been committed. We are the enforcers of the law, correct?"

"I'm telling you, that's a lousy idea. If we stir things up, the chief will be real unhappy. Have you ever seen Mitch Rainbolt unhappy? Trust me, you don't want to."

Daisy shook her head while considering Roscoe's words. She didn't know Mitch very well, that much was true. Still, the idea of letting the prankster go without even a stern warning didn't set with her either. She'd vowed to uphold the law, not look the other way.

She stared out the window as Roscoe pointed the vehicle down Main Street. Poking the bear who was trying to save her job might not be in her best interest. This was definitely a moral dilemma to which she'd have to give some thought and prayer. Shooting herself in the foot was never a good plan.

Chapter Five

He should have called first. Mitch drummed his fingers on the steering wheel of his pickup truck. Maybe she'd believe he was "just in the neighborhood." Which would be the truth, if his neighborhood was ten miles closer and he was on duty. Despite the fact that it was seven o'clock on a Friday night, he had good news and the first person he wanted to share it with was Daisy, because she deserved that much.

Was it to assuage his guilty conscience? Or because he wanted to relieve a little of the stress on her shoulders? Then again, maybe he just wanted to be the one to tell her something that would make her smile. All of the above, if he was honest with himself.

Mitch stepped out of the truck and glanced around. The minivan was parked in the drive, but it was quiet, with only the sound of a lonely cicada calling.

He strode up the gravel drive and turned the corner toward the back of the house, where a ladder was propped against the clapboard. Daisy stood on the very top platform of a weathered wooden ladder.

She wore paint-stained overalls, a tie-dyed fluorescent shirt and a faded red ball cap backward on her head. Her hair had been pulled into a low ponytail. The whole picture reminded him once again that he was old enough to be... Well, he was old.

When he got closer, he could see that she had one

gloved hand splayed against the clapboard while the other stretched to reach a cracked dormer window.

His heart lurched.

"What are you doing?" he asked.

She didn't acknowledge him, but continued to stretch. Then he noticed the earbuds.

Mitch stared for a minute while he tried to figure out how to get her attention without scaring her off the already precarious perch. Oblivious to his presence, she continued to tiptoe her fingers toward the glass.

A fraction of a second later, a screwdriver bounced off a ladder rail and hit two steps in its descent toward Mitch. He jumped aside.

Daisy yanked out the earbuds and turned, causing the ladder to wobble yet again.

"Careful!" Mitch reached out a hand to hold a rung.

"Chief? I mean, Mitch." She scrambled down the steps and pulled off her yard gloves. "I didn't know you were there. Did I hit you?"

"Close, but no. I tried to let you know I was here," he said.

"Sorry. Earbuds. I wear them so I can hear if the nanny cam goes off inside the house. It pings on my phone to let me know when the children are on the move."

He glanced up at the house. "Were you trying to get yourself killed?"

"Of course not." She crossed her arms. "Seth knocked a baseball into the dormer window. I was attempting to sort of push the glass back into place."

"I'll take care of that for you."

She frowned. "I can handle a simple window."

"I'm sure you can, except you aren't tall enough and neither is that ladder."

Daisy glanced up and seemed to consider his offer. "Well…"

"Give me five minutes. I'll measure the pane. You can put in an order for the glass at the hardware store. They'll even send someone out to replace it if you ask."

"Is that necessary? I thought pushing the glass back into place would suffice for now."

"Looks to me like a strong wind could knock it out. If we get a good summer rain, you're going to have more than air coming in."

A grimace marred her features, and she closed her eyes as if reconciling herself to his words. "Note to self. Move window repair to the top of a never-ending to-do list."

"Come on. I'm not doing anything right now. Why not at least allow me to do a temporary patch and measure the pane for you?"

"All right. Thanks."

"Have you got a tape measure?"

Daisy disappeared into the house and came back a moment later with a carpenter's tape measure.

"Perfect." Mitch repositioned the ladder, tucked the tape measure in his pocket and climbed to the top step. When he pulled the tape measure out of his pocket, the ladder wobbled and creaked.

"Oh!" Daisy reached both hands out to firmly grasp the rails.

"It's fine. It held you, didn't it?"

"Don't take offense, but you've got more bulk than I do, and the ladder is as old as the house. I really don't want to have to explain to Henna or Roscoe why you're unconscious in my backyard when I call 911."

Mitch chuckled. "Good point." He measured the window, and then took out his camera and snapped a few shots.

"Why are you taking pictures?"

He glanced down at her. "Kind of an odd size. I'll take it with me to be sure we get the correct piece."

Hands on hips, she stared up at him with that determined expression on her face. "I thought I was going to do that."

"I stop by the hardware store nearly every day. It's no big deal." He stretched the tape measure and made a note of the length and width in his phone.

"What's that sound?" Daisy asked.

"What sound?" Mitch kept measuring.

"Are you humming?" she asked.

He froze and met her gaze. "Am I?" It spoke volumes that he was comfortable enough around her to be humming. Except that his brothers often warned him that his musical abilities were frightening.

She nodded. "It sounded like 'Amazing Grace.'"

"Could be, I guess." He did his best to appear nonchalant. With the snap of the tape measure closing, he dared to glance at her once again. "Was I off-key?"

"No," she stammered when their gazes met and held.

"That's a relief. Normally I try to wait until I know someone better before I humiliate myself."

Daisy smiled. "Good plan in theory."

"You want to throw me that duct tape?" Mitch asked.

"That's probably not a good idea. Seth and I have the same pitching skills."

Mitch tried not to laugh as he climbed down the steps. When she offered him the tape, he noted the short practical nails. His gaze moved to her face. Everything about her was practical, except her wild hair. Even with a ball cap, the springy tendrils seemed to float like they had a mind of their own. Just like Daisy.

"What?" she asked.

"Nothing."

She dropped the tape into his palm, offering an almost shy smile.

"Thanks," he murmured before taking the steps back

up the ladder. Tearing the tape, he placed even pieces along the cracks and carefully smoothed the silver material with his hand. "What do you think?" He stepped down to the ground and assessed his handiwork. "That should do the trick."

"Thank you."

"I'll get that order in."

"I am very appreciative," Daisy said. "But we agree that I am totally capable of putting in my own order. Correct?"

"Yep." He nodded. "I live around the block from the hardware store. Just saving you a trip into town." He avoided her eyes. Yeah, just saving her a trip and trying to help the woman who didn't want anyone's help.

"That's right. I forgot you mentioned that you live in town."

"I do, and I never have to worry about making it to the office during inclement weather."

"That explains a lot."

"Does it?"

"Yes. It explains why you're always the first one in."

"Monitoring my attendance?"

Daisy released a soft breath, and her face pinked. "No. I like to get into work early and I...well, I've noticed that I have never been able to beat you in."

"A little competitive?"

"That's a given."

He laughed and folded up the ladder. "Where do you want this?"

"Leave it. I'll put it away later." She gestured toward the house. "May I offer you a slice of pie while you explain how you happened to be around when I needed assistance?"

"I'm all in for pie, but in truth, I nearly forgot why I was here when I saw you on that ladder," he admitted.

"Oh, come on, you weren't really concerned, were you?"

"Yeah, I was." Mitch followed her into the house, where she pulled her cap off her head and tossed it on a coat rack in the hall. "And I stopped by because Henna picked up the curriculum for the self-defense class from the printer. I've got them all bound and ready to go in my trunk."

"You could have brought them to class tomorrow."

"Sure but if an emergency came up and I was late, then you'd be without them."

"You aren't planning on an emergency, are you?"

"I'm the chief. It happens."

"I appreciate your foresight." She headed down a short hall to the kitchen.

"I also thought you should hear the good news from me."

Daisy stopped short in the middle of the kitchen, and he nearly ran into her.

"Whoa, careful there," he said as she turned around.

"There's good news?"

"The town council met this afternoon. They've green-lighted the community center project. If we can keep it running with volunteers and donations until city elections in November, a bill for permanent funding will be on the ballot."

"That's wonderful news."

"Puts us closer to turning in a report that will show we deserve the county funds."

"You can't imagine what a relief this is, even if it is only one small obstacle overcome. I don't know what I'll do if I have to uproot those kids again."

When she met his gaze, his stomach knotted at the flash of vulnerability he saw. He knew what it was like to live on broken glass.

"I told you that I won't let that happen," he said.

"Mitch," she said, "so far you've been a terrific boss, and I count you as a new friend." She paused.

"Uh-oh. The dreaded 'but' is coming."

"No." She shook her head. "It's not like that. I want you to understand that this is not your burden."

"I got you into this mess."

"Not really, and I apologize for my behavior last Friday. I was tired and overwhelmed."

"An apology is unnecessary." He couldn't help but notice that her eyes became a darker shade of blue when she was worked up.

"Mitch, are you listening to me?"

"Absolutely."

"I am telling you that I covet your prayers regarding this situation. However, you are not responsible. I'm trusting that God has my back."

"I hear you," he said. "Truth is, I've always had a hard time turning things over to Him if I think I can handle it myself."

Daisy's eyes rounded, and a short laugh erupted. "Police chief Mitch Rainbolt, micromanaging God. Why am I not surprised?"

"I'm working on it."

She nodded toward the cozy kitchen table setup. "Have a seat."

"Thanks." Mitch ran a hand over his brow. "Warm in here," he observed.

"The central air has been arguing with me. We've got fans going in all the bedrooms."

"I can take a look at it."

Daisy gave him the palm. "I've got this." She turned to the sink and washed her hands.

"What is it about me helping you that bothers you?"

"What?" She met his gaze.

"Is it me personally?" Mitch tried to read what was

going on behind her blue eyes, which were now dark with emotion.

She released a sigh and leaned against the counter. "It's not personal. Can we leave it at that?"

"Sure." For now, Mitch silently amended as he glanced around. "Awfully quiet here."

"Big Friday night at the Anderson house. Seth and Grace were invited to a birthday party. My grandmother wore the other children out by setting up an old-fashioned sprinkler on the lawn. They're asleep."

"Wore your grandmother out too, I bet."

"She has unlimited energy. One of her new friends came and picked her up for book club."

"That's great." He smiled. "I like your grandmother. Reminds me a bit of my mom."

"My grandmother raised my sister and me when my father died. The woman is a rock."

"Everyone needs a rock in their lives." His life would have been a whole lot easier if he'd had one.

"Yes." She stared at him for a moment. "And some people simply fill the calling, don't they?"

"I suppose so." He stared right back. Was she referring to him? Nah, she was talking generalities.

"How did vacation Bible school go?" he finally asked.

"You were right. It was just what the twins needed. They made so many friends, and now they're excited about school in the fall."

"I'm glad." He glanced around, noting the big farmhouse table surrounded by six chairs and two high chairs. "How are the kittens working out?"

"Star and Rascal are assimilating to our household nicely. Right now they're in a pet play yard in the twins' room."

"A pet play yard?"

"Yes." She reached for a dish towel. "You'd be surprised

at how many places there are for kittens to hide in this house. We let them roam when they can be supervised, and when they can't, we move the play yard to wherever the most activity is. They have toys and scratch poles and a litter box and water in there. Works out nicely."

"I just learned something new."

She met his gaze. "So Henna has the car wash scheduled?"

"Next Sunday after the second service. In the church parking lot," Mitch said. "High school kids are all signed up."

"What about Rebel Ranch?"

"Reece is totally on board. Henna will get an ad in *The Weekly Rebel* for the fund-raising dinner, and Luna is handling the details of catering the meal. Roscoe already has a lead on a western band."

"When is the event?"

"End of July. The Rebel PD will be in attendance."

"Is that an order?"

"It is. Not that I have any interest in another social event, but this is our event. All part of getting that funding."

"Speaking of the department," she said. "Any leads on the cherub case?"

"It's not a case. It's a prank." Mitch frowned. He'd spent a lifetime distancing himself and his siblings from their impoverished beginnings. He refused to let an annoying prank become the Rainbolt family legacy.

"Maybe it's time to bring in the Feds." Daisy's eyes sparkled with amusement.

"Real funny." Mitch crossed his arms. "I don't know if Roscoe mentioned that we like to keep that whole situation quiet. Every time the local paper gets wind of things, they manage to make our department look like Keystone Kops."

"Oh, that's what he was trying to tell me in his eloquent way."

"Yeah. Just ride it out."

"I'll do my best. However, just riding it out is counterintuitive to the laws I am sworn to uphold."

"It's a statue, Daisy. They can be purchased at the outlet garden center in Tulsa for ten bucks. Odds are that cherub has been replaced half a dozen times over the years."

"Understood."

"Really?"

"For now."

"Can we talk about something else? Please."

"Absolutely." She opened the fridge. "Lemon meringue? My grandmother took the rest of the pies to her meeting."

"I'm not particular, but lemon meringue does happen to be my favorite."

"Mine too." She grabbed two bottles of water from the fridge and slid them onto the table.

"Thanks." His gaze spanned the room, taking in the cracked linoleum and the shag carpet visible from the living room. "This place hasn't changed much. Mrs. Kendall called those colors *Brady Bunch* green and *Partridge Family* mustard yellow."

"You've been here before?"

"Lots of times. It was owned by the Kendalls. When my mother passed, Mrs. Kendall would watch my siblings while I picked up night classes at the community college in Tulsa and worked a couple of jobs."

"You make me feel like a slacker."

"Not at all. Although, a few times I did run smack-dab into myself coming and going."

"How could you afford childcare?"

"Our own bartering system, you could say. We did chores around here. I had Reece and Tucker doing yard work. There's a peach and apple orchard out back. We helped with the harvest every year." He shrugged. "Mostly the Kendalls helped us out of the kindness of their hearts."

Daisy offered a sympathetic nod as she cut the pie. "How old were you and your siblings when you lost your mother?"

"I was twenty-one, which was the only reason child services didn't step in. Reece was sixteen, Tucker twelve, Kate eight and Levi five."

"And your father?" She slid a dessert plate laden with a thick slice of pie and a fork and napkin in front of him.

"He was gone more than not, and once my mother wasn't around to wrangle him home, he simply stopped coming around." Mitch said the words as though reciting lines from a history book. He'd learned long ago to detach himself from the pain of his mother's death and his father's desertion. It was the only way he could put one foot in front of the other and take care of his siblings.

"I'm sorry you had to deal with that."

"It all works out." He picked up his fork while eyeing Daisy, wondering how she could possibly understand.

"It does, doesn't it? Whether we like it or not. When my father was killed, my mother took off," Daisy said. "My sister and I were ten when we went to live with my grandmother." She stared out into space. "I never really understood how a parent could walk away during a time when they're needed the most."

"I gave up making sense of my father's decisions years ago." He met her gaze and searched her blue eyes for a long moment. Once again, it seemed Daisy and he had more in common than they ought to. Pain and hurt mostly. Maybe the lack of pity in the depths of those eyes explained why his mouth was running like a spigot. He hadn't talked about his mother and father in a very long time.

Daisy went to the refrigerator and removed a photo from under a collection of magnets. She handed it to him.

"My sister. This is one of my favorite pictures. It's from high school. We used to love to confuse people."

"You're a twin." Mitch peered closer, noting the matching eyes and smiles as the two young girls laughed into the camera. Even the wild halo of reddish blond hair was the same. "Identical," he continued.

"On the outside. On the inside, not so much. My sister was artistic, creative and very feminine. I'm more of a tomboy."

"Don't sell yourself short. You've got two arms and two legs and the packaging seems to be in order."

Daisy's lips twitched as she took the snapshot from his hands.

"Thank you, I think." She inspected the photo. "Either way, I look like the children's mom, which is a dilemma. How can they heal if they see her face every single day?"

"You're approaching this all wrong," he said. "Maybe the fact that you look like their mother is a blessing."

She wordlessly slid into the chair across from him, and once again disappeared into her thoughts.

As the silence stretched, Mitch bit into the lemon meringue pie. He blinked in surprise as the flavors slammed into his taste buds. "You made this?"

"You don't like it?" Alarm registered on her face.

"Daisy, this is the best pie I've ever had."

"Don't sound so surprised."

Mitch took two more bites in succession and swallowed. "Did your sister bake like this?"

She laughed. "No. She hated cooking."

He chased the last flakes of crust around the plate with his fork and looked up at her. "Tell me again—why aren't you doing this for a living?"

"When I should have, I suppose I didn't believe in myself. Now, well, now the time isn't right."

"Life is all about timing, isn't it?" He paused and

glanced at the refrigerator. "I don't suppose you'd consider seconds."

Daisy's lips curved into a slow and sweet smile before she stood and stepped to the refrigerator. "Asking a woman for seconds of her pie is a very good way to keep her smiling."

"I, uh…"

Mitch didn't have a quick comeback because it occurred to him that he liked being the guy who made Daisy smile, and that eating really delicious pie was a small price to pay for that privilege.

As she pulled open the refrigerator, he assessed her profile. She was a woman the likes of which he hadn't seen before. Smart, courageous, stubborn and beautiful. And she baked pies. The situation was becoming problematic.

"How do you think it went?" Daisy asked.

She and Mitch walked around the church classroom, straightening chairs and bringing the room back to the same order they'd found it in. With each chair she pushed in, Daisy analyzed the session she just taught.

Normally she didn't second-guess herself. After all, she had plenty of experience and she knew the material well. But this was Rebel, and it was hard to gauge an audience who spent most of its time ogling the cowboy police chief.

"I thought they were a really focused group," Mitch said.

"You did?" Daisy turned to look at him. "Seriously?"

"Yeah. And I liked that sales pitch you did at the end."

"About the community center?"

He pushed back the brim of his gray Stetson and nodded.

"That was Henna's idea. The more the citizens of Rebel associate the community center as something that involves them, the more likely they'll be to get on board."

She grabbed the box of handouts and her duty ball cap. "You know, late last night I realized that we aren't just responsible for coming up with a winning plan for the county. That plan has to actually work."

He narrowed his eyes. "What do you mean?"

"What if we don't raise the money to open the community center? Everything may look good on paper, but we have to succeed."

"Huh. And here I figured you for an eternal optimist," Mitch said. He turned off the lights, and held the door open for her as they left the classroom.

"I do consider myself an optimist. The thing is, I'm making decisions for seven now. It's not just about me." Daisy followed him down the long carpeted hall and out of the door into the late-spring sunshine. Standing on the sidewalk, she waited as he locked the church door.

"There's no reason yet to think we won't meet our goals," he said.

"Chief Rainbolt?"

Daisy and Mitch turned to find an attractive young woman from class standing behind them.

"Yes, ma'am?" Mitch queried.

"I wanted to thank you for the class. I learned a lot, especially the section on home security. Now I realize that perhaps I should have someone stop by the house to ensure that I've properly implemented the home safety protocols you outlined."

"Ma'am?"

"Of course, I'd make you dinner."

Daisy's jaw nearly dropped at the bold offer. She dared to look up at Mitch.

He stood on the sidewalk with one hand on his service weapon and the other paused in gesture. "I...um..." His mouth was open, but nothing was coming out.

"What Chief Rainbolt means," Daisy interrupted, "is

that, right now, the department is extremely busy with our participation in the new community center. However, if you'll reach out to the department on Monday, we can provide you with the contact numbers for home security companies available to assist you."

"Oh. I suppose I could do that." The woman's face fell for a brief moment. "Thank you." With a bright smile, she turned and left.

Mitch blinked and looked at Daisy. "Thank you. I'm usually right there with a response. That one caught me off guard." He met her gaze. "What's that expression on your face mean?"

"It means, I didn't realize you had groupies. That's going to be good for fund-raising." If she could tolerate giving the women of the town carte blanche to fall all over him for the summer.

"I don't have groupies," Mitch returned.

"Oh, yes. You do," she scoffed. "Surely you look in the mirror on occasion. You're single and handsome. You wear a uniform that includes a Stetson. Women swoon over that stuff."

"All women?" He narrowed his eyes.

Daisy's face warmed at his scrutiny. "Most women." She prayed that he couldn't see the truth in her eyes, because, yes, she was one of those women. The admission irked her constantly.

"I see." He moved closer. "Let me carry that box for you."

"I've got it."

"This is an old-fashioned town, Daisy. I'm the police chief. It looks bad if you're carrying a heavy box and I'm not helping."

She released a breath.

"Let me be chivalrous, would you?"

"Fine." Daisy released the box.

As they passed the drugstore, Daisy paused to read the sign in the window. "Rebel Ranch Fishing Derby. Seth and Grace keep talking about that. They're too young this year. Maybe next year."

"You can still take them fishing," he said.

"I could. If I knew how to fish."

"Can they swim?"

"I have no idea." Daisy looked up at Mitch and grimaced. "It appears that not only am I a naive homeowner, but my mothering skills are questionable too."

"Cut yourself some slack, Daisy. It's not like the shooting range. There isn't a test. What you're doing with the kids is on-the-job training."

"What if I fail?" In her heart she knew there was no way she'd be a match for her sister. Deb had been born with the maternal gene. Daisy had not.

"You pick yourself up and try again." He shrugged. "Can you swim?"

"Yes."

"Great. The two of us can handle the situation."

Daisy looked up at him. "What situation?"

"Pay attention. We're talking about fishing. You and I are going to take the twins fishing."

She released a small gasp. "I don't know the first thing about how to fish."

"I'll teach you."

She stared at him, astonished at the offer. "Why would you do that?"

"You just said—"

"Mitch, you can't go around fixing things for everyone."

"Not everyone. You're new to Rebel, and you're in my employ. I've lived here all my life. I'm offering my expertise in areas unknown to you."

"What am I doing in return?"

"Teaching a class."

She was silent for several moments, considering his words as they continued to walk down the street. "About the fishing?"

"Oh, so you are interested."

"Yes. The kids deserve this opportunity. That's why we moved here."

"Is it so hard to accept help from me?"

"No. I told you. It's not personal."

"Right."

She looked up at him. "Should I get poles and such?"

"Do you know what 'and such' is?"

"Not a clue."

He laughed and adjusted the box in his arms. "I have both the poles and the 'and such' covered. How about next Saturday?"

"We have class the next two Saturdays."

"Fishing is in the morning. Class isn't till the afternoon."

"Okay. We can do that."

"Bring sunscreen, water and hats. I'll bring the rest."

She nodded, mentally creating a list. "Got it."

"I'll pick you up at 5:00 a.m."

Daisy's head jerked back, and her jaw slacked. "Five a.m.!"

"I thought you liked being the first one in."

"Yes. In the morning. Five a.m. is practically the middle of the night."

"The sun rises at five thirty. Fish bite better at dawn. So the earlier the better."

"Why?"

"What do you mean, why?"

"Why do fish bite better so early?"

Mitch nodded to a group of elderly women who passed them on the sidewalk before turning back to Daisy.

"Once the sun's rays penetrate the water and warm things up, fish slow down and are more difficult to catch. It's siesta time for them, and they're not as interested in the bait. We want to catch them hungry and eating insects on the water's surface in the early hours."

"Don't the fish like to sleep in on the weekend?"

"Uh, no."

She stopped walking and stared at him. "Is this all true, or are you making it up because I'm a city girl?"

When he started laughing, she found herself fascinated by how the simple act softened his features. Mitch was normally so starched and serious about everything.

"What's so funny?"

"You really are a city girl."

"I am, and I'm going to tell that tale to Seth and Grace when I drag them out of bed in the middle of the night."

"It'll be fun."

"That's what people always say when they try to convince you to do something you know is not going to be fun." She shook her head. "I'll be ready at five because they deserve this wonderful opportunity to experience nature, but I'm bringing lots of coffee."

"Deal."

When he stopped on the curb in front of her minivan, she pulled her keys from her pocket and hit the remote unlock button.

"How do you like driving a minivan?" Mitch asked.

"I used to drive a cute little hybrid that could hit sixty miles per hour in less than seven and a half seconds." She sighed, remembering her sweet ride. She'd give it up again for her sister's kids, but that didn't take the sting out of the memory.

"Zero to sixty. I don't want to know how you know that."

"Please. It nearly killed me to trade it in. I used the

small life insurance policy my brother-in-law had for this very boring yet top-of-the-line safety-rated vehicle with a zillion airbags and for the down payment on the five-bedroom farmhouse fixer-upper. The children's monthly checks from Uncle Sam are put away for their education."

"That was smart, but it couldn't hurt to spend a little on the house repairs."

"No. Once I dip into their education fund, that's how it starts. There will always be a good reason to take money out. Then it's gone."

"Why do I think you speak from experience?" he asked.

"You would be correct. My mother emptied our college funds little by little. Like you, my sister and I juggled several jobs to get through college."

"Made you a better person, right?"

She released a short, bitter laugh. "That's one way to look at things. But you have to consider that I now have five kids who might want to go to college. A college savings account will come in handy in ten years."

"Maybe they won't want to go to college."

"Fine by me. The money is theirs. At least they'll have choices. Something I didn't have."

"You've thought this through."

"I have. Many sleepless nights."

He slid the box into the van. "Any big plans for the rest of the day?"

"I'm supposed to meet Luna at the Jeep place." She glanced around. "What exactly is the Jeep place?"

"End of the block and turn right on Second Street. Across the street from the new library. Beep Jeep Tours. They take tourists around the lake and on sightseeing excursions. Big deal in the autumn for foliage tours."

"I guess I can see that."

"Tell Luna hello from me."

"I will, and, Mitch…" Daisy met his gaze and nearly faltered when his dark eyes searched hers.

"Yeah?"

"Thanks for not having an emergency elsewhere today."

"I enjoyed the class. You're a good instructor, and somehow you managed to make me look good too."

"Chief, you did that all by yourself." Daisy armed the car alarm, and offered a two-finger salute as she headed down the street.

She didn't dare say more for fear she'd be just as bad as his groupies. It wasn't Mitch's fault that he was handsome on the outside and a nice guy on the inside, she reminded herself. Still, she refused to become the president of his local fan club.

Passing Rebel Vet and Rescue, she glanced in. There were two entrances, one for dogs and one for cats. Both waiting rooms were visible from the street, and they were full. Tucker Rainbolt had a very robust business.

At the corner, she turned right and passed the new library building. On the other side was Beep Jeep Tours, and next to that an empty storefront. Daisy cupped her hands to peek inside. The sun streaming through the windows reflected off glass display cases. A bakery?

"Daisy!"

She turned at Luna's voice. She smiled as the petite chef approached wearing stylish red capris and a print blouse.

"So nice to see you, again. I met your lovely grandmother."

"You did?"

"Yes. At the book club last night." She put both hands over Daisy's. "I love your pies."

"Oh?" Daisy stared, dumbfounded. Chef Luna Diaz loved her pies!

"The key lime berry. Oh, my heart, be still." She

grinned. "The French apple is a close second. The crumb topping on that one. I'm still dreaming about it."

"Thank you."

Luna nodded toward the empty storefront. "Do you like the shop?"

"Was this a bakery?"

"Yes. It's been empty a long time."

"If only we could go inside."

"We can." Luna pulled a ring of keys from her purse and jangled them. "I own the building."

A giddy bubble stirred inside Daisy. Going into a bakery, even an empty one, was an exciting prospect.

When Luna unlocked the door and pushed it open, tiny bells tinkled a melodic greeting. Mesmerized, Daisy followed her into the shop.

"No electricity but I'll take care of that."

Daisy released a sound of delight as she crossed the threshold. A twin set of suspended schoolhouse light fixtures hung in the front of the shop. Dust sparkles danced through the air, swirling in and out of a stream of light from the big display window that helped illuminate the space.

The square footage of the shop was much larger than it appeared from the outside. One wall was entirely composed of what was probably the original faded red brick. The wall reached up to meet an oak-beamed ceiling, with two large industrial ceiling fans in the front and back of the shop.

Traditional display cases and a large glass counter with an antique cash register greeted customers. The floor was checkerboard tiles.

This place. It was as though she'd been waiting for this place her whole life. Daisy moved behind the counter and looked out at the sidewalk and the street. Then she skimmed her fingers over the keys of the cash register. "What's the story here?"

"The same story for many small businesses in town. Family owned for years. The kids weren't interested in staying in Rebel."

"That's a shame."

"I agree. We're going to use the space for a pop-up shop for the bake sale," Luna said. "Rebel Roasters has had success with this model."

"Have you thought about actually opening a bakery?" Daisy asked.

"I have my finger in too many other pies." Luna chuckled. "Good joke, *sí*?"

"Yes." Daisy laughed.

"It's the truth. Right now, I handle the guest ranch and run a catering business. There is no time for another project." She turned to Daisy and cocked her head. "Perhaps you'd like to run a bakery for me?"

"Wh-what?" Daisy clutched her hands together.

"You could manage this bakery."

Daisy couldn't move, couldn't answer for a long moment. "Another time and place, I would say yes. This is my dream."

"Why haven't you followed your dream before now?"

"I ask myself that question all the time," Daisy murmured. Deep inside she knew the answer. Fear. Plain and simple.

"We will leave it in God's hands. I have owned this building for two years, waiting for the right person to open a bakery. I would finance the operation, and they would run the shop." She touched Daisy's arm. "I believe you are that person. But it must be God's timing."

"Yes." Daisy could only nod while she worked to process what Luna said.

"For now, I have a cleaning service from Tulsa coming

in this week. Since we are not cooking or eating on the premises, we don't need any licensing. We'll put a banner outside, and place an ad in the paper and in the church bulletin. The ranch will let their guests know." She smiled. "That's all there is to it. We will plan to open the shop for limited hours with your pies and my pastries."

"Your pastries. Mmm, what kind?"

"Chocolate-almond croissants, coconut-crust raspberry tarts and perhaps my cinnamon sticky buns."

"I'm drooling already." Daisy's gaze spanned the shop. "This is so exciting."

"It is, and there is a room in the back where the children can play if you want to bring them along."

"That's wonderful."

"*Sí.* And perhaps once you are here, you will not want to leave."

"I already feel that way."

Luna chuckled. "Now for the big question. Do you have time to produce enough pies? I predict that they will be in great demand."

"If we can sell them, I can bake them. It's late June. The peaches and apples in my yard will be ready to harvest soon."

"I'll take some for my pastries."

"Yes. Absolutely."

Luna glanced at her watch. "I must leave. I have another appointment." She smiled at Daisy. "Maybe you'd like to stay a few more minutes?"

"Could I?"

"Oh, yes. Lock the door behind you."

"Thank you."

"I'll email you and we can discuss hours. Maybe we can find someone to help us."

"Officer McFarland expressed an interest. I'll ask him."

"Excellent choice. He loves my pâte à choux."

"Oh?"

"Yes. I teach cooking and baking classes at the ranch in the off-season. Roscoe is always in attendance. He's quite good."

"Yes. He is," Daisy said. "Roscoe is quite a guy, and I may have underestimated him."

Luna laughed. "I can understand how that might happen." With a hand on the door, she turned to Daisy once more. "Close your eyes and pretend you manage this bakery. I can see it. Can you?"

Daisy smiled as the door opened and the chimes offered a delicate encore to Luna's departure. Her heart began a steady thump, thump, thump. Closing her eyes, she imagined her pies in the glass cases and on crystal pedestal plates on the counters. Pies. Her pies. The meringue would be piled high and lightly browned at the top of the swirl. Blackberry pies with a golden lattice, the juice peeking through around the plump berries. Peach, apple and pumpkin all waiting for eager customers.

She visualized her name on the awning outside. *Daisy's Pies.*

The front window would feature an eye-catching display to make passersby slow down and take a peek. Unable to resist, they'd step inside.

Daisy smiled and opened her eyes. Could her dreams ever become a reality when she had the responsibility of five beautiful children in her life? Managing a bakery meant three o'clock mornings, and twelve-hour shifts. An impossibility with the demands of motherhood.

The words on a scripture card in her Bible came to her along with a calm reassurance. "The Lord will fulfill his purpose for me."

"I give this to You, Lord," she whispered.

Chapter Six

The sun made an appearance on the horizon as Mitch guided his pickup along the Rebel Ranch north entrance.

"Everyone still awake back there?" he asked.

"We are," Grace called from the backseat of the pickup.

Seth popped his head between the front seat's headrests. "Where are we going fishing, Mr. Mitch?"

"We're there."

"That sign says Rebel Ranch," Seth replied.

"That's right." Mitch parked the truck and turned in his seat to address the young boy. "The ranch has a stocked pond. That means they put the fish in there for us."

"They do?" His blue eyes rounded with wonder.

Next to him, Grace silently followed the conversation, her dark eyes moving back and forth.

They were good kids, courteous, articulate and soft-spoken. About the same age as Kate when Mitch took over the care of his family. The surprise was that today's excursion had stirred up some good memories. He'd thought all he had were the painful ones.

"A pond stocked for fishing. That's a very odd phenomenon," Daisy murmured from the front passenger seat.

"It's a guest ranch, everything is about the guests. Reece hired someone to monitor the water quality, oxygen content, water temperatures, stocking densities, species selection and restocking. Pond management is a science."

"I guess so." She yawned and stretched.

Mitch reached for his travel mug before he got out of the truck, then went around to open Daisy's door. "Have you ever cleaned a fish?" he asked.

"I'm sure I could if I tried." She met his gaze. Blue eyes peeked out from beneath the brim of the ridiculous olive-drab fishing hat on her head.

He tried to keep a straight face as he continued. "Is that a yes or a no?"

"Truthfully, outside of a restaurant, the only fish I've ever spent time with were wrapped in white paper and came from the fish market."

Mitch laughed. "I guess that's a no."

"Why did you ask?"

"I wanted to know who was cleaning today's catch. Me or you."

"Oh, sorry. I'm definitely washing the dishes."

"Works for me." In fact, it all worked for him. The idea of cleaning fish while Daisy did the dishes made him smile. He pulled a faded ball cap from his backpack and slapped it on. "Does everyone have sunblock on?"

"Sunblock." Daisy pulled it from her backpack and handed it to the twins before slathering the white lotion on her own exposed skin. Then she faced him. "Okay. I'm ready."

"There's a blob on your chin." Mitch wiped it off with the pad of his finger a second before his good sense kicked in. Touching Daisy was not a good idea. Even sitting close to the woman in a vehicle did something to his sensory processing, causing his hands to fumble and his tongue to trip over itself.

"Thank you," she murmured. Her gaze remained fixed on the bottle in her hands. "I'm working on freckle mitigation."

"I like your freckles."

Her face pinked. "That makes two of you. My grandmother says freckles are a ginger's superpower."

Mitch stared at the sprinkling of copper across her nose and scattered over her shoulders. So that was the secret lure she had over him. Freckles.

He quickly moved to the back of the truck and picked up the cooler and the tackle box. Then he elbowed the tailgate shut.

"Seth. Grace," he called. "Grab your gear, and don't forget the life vests. Be sure your sneakers are tied so you don't trip."

"Yes, Mr. Mitch." They said the words in unison.

"Follow me," he said.

Daisy race walked to keep up with him. "You do that really well."

"Do what?"

"Take command." She glanced over her shoulder. "They're following you like soldiers."

"As they should. Fishing is serious business, and we're running late."

In the distance birds chirped and a flock of herons soared across the sky. Mitch took the long way to the pier, instead of down the muddy incline. The ground crunched beneath their feet as they walked a path blanketed with fallen pine needles, no doubt alerting the wildlife of their arrival. Overhead a screeching bird filled the air.

"What was that?" Grace asked.

"Red-tailed hawk. We may have chased off his snack," Mitch said.

"Really?" Seth asked.

"Really," Mitch returned.

Tall, lush conifers stood like sentries, forming a line to guide them along the path. The trees stretched high into an endless blue sky that chased off the pink-and-burgundy streaks of sunrise. Even the humidity had cooperated today.

The air was a few degrees warmer than crisp. That was rare for late June, which usually heralded the oppressive heat of an Oklahoma summer.

"What a perfect morning," Daisy breathed.

She was right.

As they approached, the scent of pond filled his senses—dampness and algae along with the faint smell of late blooming lilacs. He inhaled deeply, hoping to capture the calming perfume.

When they rounded the bend, Rebel Ranch pond came into sight. Lined on one side by weeping willows whose wispy, ground-sweeping branches skimmed the surface, the water was so clear he could see right to the bottom in places. Mitch glanced on either side of the pier, checking for weeds. Deciding there were less on the right, he set up there.

"Oh, it's so beautiful," Daisy said. "Huge. It's not what I imagined a pond to be."

"Rebel Ranch pond is a little over an acre."

"That's a big pond."

"Good sized. When it's not tourist season, I camp down here." Mitch's gaze skittered across the water to a protected area formed by a cluster of maples, where he'd usually set up his tent. Each night the sounds of nature lulled him to sleep. Each morning he drank a cup of coffee and silently prayed as he stood on the water's edge.

"I've never been camping," Daisy said.

"You're kind of a low maintenance gal. You'd like it."

Daisy stared at him for a moment. "I'll take that as a compliment."

Mitch placed the cooler and tackle box down on the wooden planks of the pier. Slipping the backpack from his shoulders, he sat down. Then he rolled up the legs of his jeans and took off his socks and sneakers.

"Is that part of catching fish?" Seth asked.

"No. This is part of relaxing. Watch and learn." He

looked straight ahead. "See those bugs flying over the water there?"

"Yes."

"They just scattered. That usually indicates that there are fish right below the surface. Maybe a whole school of them parked there." He opened his tackle box. "We'll cast there first."

"Cast?" Seth asked.

"I'm generally talking about tossing the bait in the water using a rod. We can talk spinners and casting rods next trip." Mitch turned to Seth and Grace. "Have a seat on the pier and put on those life vests. They are to be worn at all times. You two might lose your balance and fall in."

Seth and Grace scrambled to obey.

"Let's start with your pole," he said to Daisy. He took the pole from her hands and carefully baited the line with a rubber worm.

"Is that a fake worm?"

"Artificial lures and flies are the only things allowed on the pond." He glanced at her. "You know how to cast a rod?"

She arched a brow. "Maybe I wasn't clear. I've never been this close to a fishing pole in my entire life."

He chuckled. "Watch." Mitch stood and pulled back. The line sailed through the air before landing on the water. He handed it back to Daisy.

"Wow, that was cool," Seth said.

Mitch grinned at the enthusiasm on the youngster's face. Maybe Tucker was right. He needed to remember more good stuff like the first time he took his siblings fishing. The day was not unlike this one.

Once he'd cast another line, he offered the pole to Seth. "It's yours for today. But be careful. It's my favorite. Used to belong to my brother."

Levi's pole. Somehow it seemed right. Mitch didn't know why, and he was hesitant to overthink the sentiment.

"Yes, sir, I will." Seth assessed the rod and grinned at his sister while Mitch proceeded to prepare the next pole and cast the lure into the water.

"This one's yours, Grace."

She raised her face and offered him a sweetly shy smile. "Thank you, Mr. Mitch."

"Yes. Thank you, Mr. Mitch," Daisy said. She saluted him with her travel coffee mug.

"There's more coffee in there, along with muffins. Do you want one?" He nodded toward his backpack.

"You have muffins?" Daisy's blue eyes lit up.

"Blueberry. From Eagle Donuts."

"Say no more." Daisy wasted no time rifling through his pack and offering everyone a plump, sugar-sprinkled muffin. "Napkins?" she asked.

"We don't need napkins out here, city girl."

"Right." Daisy pulled a tissue from her own backpack and set her muffin down on it.

Mitch chuckled. "I take back what I said about camping."

"Decorum is what separates us from the animals."

"I thought it was opposable thumbs," he returned.

"What do we do now, Mr. Mitch?" Grace asked.

"We eat these really good muffins, and let the fish do their part."

"That's all?" Seth asked.

"Part of fishing is knowing how to relax. And less talking. It scares the fish."

Daisy yawned again. "What if I fall asleep?"

"Not a problem. Just don't let go of your pole. Wedge it between the plank spaces on the pier, and the fish will holler when he's ready to be reeled in."

She stared at him. "You're joking, right?"

"Am I?" Mitch baited his own pole, and cast it out a distance before he sat down on the pier between Daisy and the twins.

"This is nice." Daisy said the words softly, and glanced toward her niece and nephew. "Look how happy they are."

He followed Daisy's gaze to Seth and Grace. The siblings sat on the pier, their knobby-kneed, skinny legs swinging back and forth while they quietly chattered.

"You did this, Mitch. Thank you."

Happy? Was that the emotion that sat on his chest and clogged his throat when he glanced at the twins and Daisy? Or was it contentment? Either way, he knew it wasn't about the fish.

When he raised his face to the warming sun, a movement caught his attention. Mitch glanced across the pond to where the bushes shivered, and a mother deer and her fawn eased to the edge of the water for a drink. "Look."

"A deer," Daisy murmured. "Seth, Grace. Look over there."

"Quietly," Mitch said. "We don't want to scare the deer or the fish."

"You have deer in Oklahoma?" Seth asked.

Mitch chuckled and ruffled Seth's hair. "Sure we do. They like to hang out in traffic sometimes, which can be a real problem."

"Uh-oh." Daisy's eyes popped open wide. "Something's tugging on my line."

"Hold it steady," Mitch said.

"I need help," she whispered, her voice panicked.

Mitch wedged his own pole between the pier's planks. When he reached around Daisy with an arm, she continued to pull the line until her back rested against his chest. For a moment he froze, realizing she was in his arms. Then he shook off the panic.

"We got it," he soothed. "This one's feisty, but he isn't large."

"What do I do?"

His hands covered her smaller ones on the pole. "Hang on. We're going to slowly reel him in."

Daisy tensed.

"You're doing fine," he murmured. A moment later the trout popped out of the water, all the while struggling against the line.

"Look, Aunt Daisy," Grace said. "You caught a fish."

"Easy," Mitch said. "We aren't done yet." He continued the steady motion of reeling until the fish hovered over the pier.

"Aunt D, you really did it," Seth said.

"This is so cool," Grace added.

"Oh, he's looking at us." Daisy grimaced and turned away, disengaging herself from Mitch.

"Mr. Fish is getting a kick out of the fact that he's your first catch. I'll take your picture. You have bragging rights now."

Daisy paused as if considering his words. "Maybe I should get a picture." She pulled her phone from her pants pocket and passed it to him. "Sure. Okay." Excitement laced her voice. "But only because my grandmother will never believe I caught a fish."

Mitch chuckled as he snapped her picture and handed the phone back. Then he took the pole once again. "Now, let's get this guy back in the water." He carefully removed the hook and tossed the fish into the pond.

"Why did you do that?" Daisy asked, her eyes round with surprise.

"Mighty as he was, that trout was appetizer-sized. I'm waiting for a meal. We catch and release anything smaller than fourteen inches. Ranch rules."

"That was fun though, wasn't it?" She grinned, her eyes aglow with delight.

He couldn't help smiling back. The pure joy on Daisy's

face caught him by surprise. It wrapped around his heart and squeezed.

"Yeah. It was." Spending time with Daisy and Seth and Grace was fun. And he hadn't had fun in a long time.

"Do you always catch fish?" she asked.

"No. It's even more enjoyable when you sit here for hours, and don't catch a thing but your peace of mind."

Daisy chuckled. "You lose your peace of mind often?"

He couldn't resist tugging on the brim of her cap. "Please. You've met Roscoe. You tell me."

"Your pole, Mr. Mitch," Seth said. "It's moving."

Mitch glanced over at his bobbing line. "It sure is." He grabbed the rod and let out the line, maintaining a steady grip. "I do believe this one is our dinner."

He turned once more to glance at Daisy. She looked as if she belonged on this pier dipping her toes in the water. Her attention moved from Grace to Seth and finally to him.

When their eyes connected, she smiled.

In a heartbeat Mitch realized that when he was around Daisy, he felt like he was home. While he meant the words, it was worrisome as the woman had only been in Rebel three weeks. He'd best be very careful, because Daisy Anderson might just reel him in if he wasn't. Mitch blinked at the idea that for the first time in his life, he was having second thoughts about fighting the line.

"Morning, Roscoe. Happy Fourth of July," Daisy said. She fastened her seat belt and adjusted her sunglasses.

"Long time no see, missy."

"The chief let me reduce my hours on the street since he couldn't pay me overtime for the classes I've given the last three weekends."

"Whole town's talking about the community center."

"That's what we want." She turned to him. "By the way,

thanks for working at the bake sale the last two Saturdays. You were a lifesaver."

"Showing up and getting first dibs on your pies and Luna's pastries is a no-brainer. Plus I get to spend time with Luna."

"Wait a minute. You like my pies? Really?"

"Right now there are ten in my freezer."

"Ten?" Daisy blinked. She was flattered, and more than a bit surprised.

"Just the fruit ones. They freeze the best."

"I...I don't know what to say."

"Well, I do. How are you baking all those pies, teaching classes, working full-time and wrangling five kids?"

"I've always believed that the Lord gives you what you need for every situation. He gave me the ability to function on four hours of sleep along with eyes in the back of my head." Which was the absolute truth most days.

"I guess." Roscoe shook his head. "So, why is it you're not with your kids at the parade today?"

"It's my regularly scheduled shift."

"Aw, Mitch would have let you off."

"I haven't been here long enough to get holidays off. I don't want preferential treatment."

"I guess it's you and me then. Gonna be a long day."

"What makes you say that? The parade is followed by the church picnic. The only other thing going on is the fireworks at dusk, and we'll both be home by then."

"I've been doing this a long time. When we get off at three, it's going to feel like we've been here a week."

"Oh, it can't be that bad."

Roscoe raised his brows and eyed her with something between sympathy and pity. "Stay hydrated. Heat index is ninety-two and the humidity is eighty-five. Rain in the forecast for tomorrow."

She raised her water bottle in the air. "Got it, but I no

longer put much faith in the meteorologist on television. He's predicted rain twice before and fired blanks."

"This one's gonna be a gully washer. Trust me. My rain knee is throbbing. It only does that when we have precipitation on the way."

"I suppose we'll see."

"Yep. In the meantime, let's get this vehicle off Main Street and do patrol before the crowds start lining up at the curb."

"Sounds good." Daisy unscrewed the lid of her water bottle and took a long swig. Roscoe was right about one thing. It was hot and humid.

Her partner checked traffic before he backed up the Crown Vic. "Heard you and the chief went fishing," he said.

At his words, water flooded Daisy's throat and she began coughing.

"You need me to pull over and do Heimlich?"

"No," she sputtered. "I'm fine." Daisy wiped her eyes and turned to Roscoe. "Who told you that?"

"Alice."

"My grandmother?" Daisy's thoughts wandered back to the fish dinner they'd all shared. True to his word, Mitch cleaned the fish, her grandmother fried it up and Daisy did the dishes. She couldn't help but let a smile escape. It had been a lovely evening. Almost like they were a family.

"Your grandmother is a beautiful woman," Roscoe mused. "I plan to invite her to lunch."

Daisy's eyes popped wide at his words. "I thought you were crushing on Luna."

"She has put me in the friend zone." He frowned at her. "And don't look so surprised. I'm talking about burgers and fries, not wedding cake and champagne."

"The age difference… It doesn't bother you?" Daisy mentally calculated that Roscoe at fifty-five was fifteen years her grandmother's junior.

"Age doesn't matter as much as most folks think. Look at you and the chief. You're nearly a decade younger than him."

"We went fishing. With the kids. We aren't dating."

"If you say so."

"I do," Daisy returned.

"I'm parking right here on First Street. We can see the crowds coming down Main and back up Rebel Avenue." He rolled down the window and stuck his head outside.

"What are you doing?" she asked.

"Smelling."

"Why?"

"I can tell if the parade is on schedule."

"Pardon me?"

"The kettle corn and funnel cake sidewalk vendors fire things up when the parade is about to begin." He inhaled deeply with his eyes closed and a smile on his face. "Yep, I smell parade, and there's roasted cinnamon pecans this year too."

Daisy followed suit and rolled down her window. When she inhaled, a waft of salty-sweet warm kettle corn reached her. The scents reminded her of the Arapahoe County fair back in Colorado. Good memories. "You're right."

"Course I am."

She scanned the parade-goers and stopped. Mitch. It was unmistakably him. Standing above the crowd, he wore a navy blue Rebel Police Department T-shirt that hugged his wide shoulders, and his favorite faded blue ball cap on his head. Her eyes lingered for a moment before moving to her grandmother and her nieces and nephews. Seth, Grace and even Christian waved miniature American flags in the air as they waited for the floats to appear. Their faces were bright with anticipation.

"Look over there," Daisy said. "The chief is standing next to my grandmother."

"Where?" Roscoe asked.

"Outside the vet office, next to the curb."

"It surely is. Those are all your kids?"

"Yes. Seth, Grace and Christian are standing next to Mitch. You've met the twins. That double stroller my grandmother is pushing has Sam and PJ."

"Almost a softball team."

"No, that would be nine."

"With you, your grandmother and Mitch, you're getting close."

Daisy jerked her head toward Roscoe.

He shrugged. "You never know. You and the chief. Maybe down the road, you'll have enough kids for a team."

"Me and the chief?" she sputtered.

"He's sweet on you. Once he gets over himself, he'll figure it out too."

"He's not sweet on…" She shook her head. "Mitch and I are friends, and you've got us married with children."

"Like I said, once he figures out that the future ain't the past, he'll be ready to handle today."

Daisy rubbed the bridge of her nose. Roscoe's unusual cheerfulness threatened to make her head explode. "Do you have any aspirin?"

"Sure, in the glove box."

Downing two aspirin with her water, she checked her watch and leaned back in the seat. Only six more hours.

When the dash phone buzzed, Roscoe hit the "accept" button. "What's up, Henna?"

"Widow Maupier's granddaughter called. Says her grandma is having another asthma attack."

"Call an ambulance."

"Granny refuses," Henna returned. "She doesn't want to bother the nice paramedics on a holiday."

Roscoe rolled his eyes. "What do you want me to do?"

"She'd like you to pick up her grandmother's inhaler and drop it off."

"Fine. I'm on my way."

"Really?" Daisy asked when he disconnected the call. "You can't be serious."

"All part of the job."

"The pharmacist will let you have her medicine? That doesn't violate the health care act or some other law?"

"It's her inhaler, and she asked me to get it. The pharmacy is actually closed, but the pharmacist will go in for this."

"Really?"

"You already said that. This is Rebel, and if you haven't figured it out by now, this town is nothing like the big city."

Daisy fastened her seat belt. "No. I guess not." And she wasn't sure how she felt about this blurring of the rules.

Roscoe turned the vehicle around, bypassed Main Street where the parade had begun, headed down Second Street and parked.

"I'll be right back. I'm going to walk over to the pharmacy. Easier than trying to get around that giant float honoring William K. Rebel."

"Who is William K. Rebel?"

"He only founded Rebel. What did you think?"

"I had no idea," Daisy murmured.

Roscoe crossed the street and strode into the pharmacy, emerging mere minutes later with a small white bag. "All right, let's get going."

"What? No lights and siren?" she asked when he backed up the vehicle. "What if we don't make it in time?"

"We will. She doesn't live far enough that lights and sirens matter. Besides, that's a surefire way to land myself on the front page of *The Weekly Rebel*. Did you read last week's issue?"

"Um. No."

"Front-page story, above the fold, was a write-up of a big robbery right here in Rebel."

"I don't recall any robbery."

"Mrs. Boerner's subscription to *Miniature Donkey Talk Magazine* was stolen from her mailbox."

She chuckled. "Okay, so not a big robbery, but still, legit."

"Mrs. Boerner forgot to renew said magazine. They cover our department with an unauthorized section they call the Police Blotter. They'll print anything to sell papers, and I won't be part of the show. Mitch feels the same way."

"You're telling me that *The Weekly Rebel* wields a lot of influence in this town?"

"Absolutely. It's not like your big city paper. Weekly papers document life in small towns. Here in Rebel, the first thing people do on Wednesday mornings is grab their Bible, their coffee and check *The Weekly Rebel*. I'm not sure which is more popular, obituaries or the Police Blotter column."

He pulled up in front of a small brick cottage on the edge of town and turned to Daisy. "I'm going to run that up to the door."

"Would you like me to?"

"Naw, I want to check on her. Let her know we're here if she needs us."

"Sure. Of course." Daisy smiled. Despite his grousing, Roscoe had an affection for the citizens of Rebel that she found endearing.

When he got back in the vehicle, Daisy glanced up. "Any problems?" she asked.

Roscoe held a plastic-wrap-covered plate of cookies aloft. "Not unless you don't like macadamia nuts."

She grinned and took the plate.

"What say we drive over to the Gas and Go to grab a couple of those fake lattes and take a cookie break?" he asked. "It's the only place open on a holiday."

"Sounds good to me."

He circled out of the neighborhood and down Second Street, driving slowly.

Daisy glanced at the empty bakery storefront with longing and then at Beep Jeep Tours.

"Roscoe, stop. Stop."

"Why?"

"Pull over. I think I saw something."

Roscoe yanked the steering wheel, and pulled the vehicle to the curb.

"Look. Up on the roof of the Jeep place. Isn't that your missing cherub?"

Roscoe yanked the ball cap off his shiny scalp, and started laughing. "So it is."

"How do you want to handle this?" Daisy asked.

"We're going up there now before the parade passes by and the whole town sees the thing and *The Weekly Rebel* gets their story."

"You want to climb onto the roof now? The parade has begun." In the distance, the sound of a marching band confirmed her words.

"Sure enough. I'm not going to let the Rebel Police Department look like a bunch of yahoos. Nope. Not on my watch."

Daisy's mind raced as she processed Roscoe's intentions. Climb on the roof? That would make her a coconspirator with her partner in whatever happened in the next few minutes. "We should call Mitch."

"The chief thinks you and I are ticket peddlers." He looked at her. "Weren't you the one who said that you wanted to enforce the law?"

"Mitch says it isn't a case." Daisy met his gaze. "And you were the one who didn't want to expend any energy on the cherub."

"This is different. It's about saving face." Roscoe glanced around, determination in his eyes. "I can tell you that whoever put that cherub up there will be monitoring the situation so they get the last laugh, and I'm not going to let that happen. The parade starts on First and Main Streets. I'll go around to the back side of that store and get our evidence before the parade turns the corner and hits Second Street."

"You don't have a ladder. Maybe you could call the fire department."

"I can climb up there."

Daisy punched in Henna's number on the dashboard phone.

"Henna, Roscoe found the cherub, and he's going to scale the roof of Beep Jeep to get it. Can you please talk some sense into him before he breaks his neck?"

"Go, Roscoe. I'm so proud of you," Henna said.

"Henna!" Daisy let out a breath of stunned surprise.

"Someone has to defend the department," Henna said. "Keep me posted, Roscoe."

Roscoe disconnected the call and removed his seat belt.

Daisy looked at her partner. "So basically, I'm the only person here who thinks this is a very bad idea?"

"Yep. But I respect your right to disagree," Roscoe said.

"This is not going to end well."

For once the cloud of generic discontent that perpetually hung over the old-timer seemed to have dissipated. A smile lifted the corners of his mouth, and there was a sparkle in his eyes.

Was she really going to try to stop him? No. This was his moment.

"Are you coming or not?" Roscoe said as he opened his door.

"Yes. Someone has to catch you."

Daisy pushed open her door and stepped out into summer's sauna. For a moment she stood staring at the pitched roof of Beep Jeep Tours, where the stone cherub wore a rope around its middle and nothing more. Mitch was not going to be pleased.

Chapter Seven

"It's your turn, Mr. Mitch." Grace scooted closer to the table, her eyes on the board-game pieces spread over Daisy's kitchen table.

When she shoved her long hair away from her face as she concentrated, Mitch smiled. The eight-year-old reminded him of his little sister Kate at that age.

"Pass that spinner over here, pal." He shifted little Sam onto his other knee, and studied the board himself.

"Will Aunt Daisy be home in time for fireworks?" Christian asked from his seat on the chair next to Mitch.

"Probably," Mitch said. In truth, he didn't have a clue. A glance at the rooster wall clock said it was five minutes since the last time he'd checked. Eight thirty. Hours past the end of Daisy's shift. He'd called in to dispatch, and they didn't report any unusual activity on her shift.

It occurred to him that she could have had a date, and he'd been mulling over that thought for the past hour, confused at the mixed emotions the idea had stirred. If he didn't know better, he might even think one of those emotions might be jealousy.

"Are you sure?" Christian continued.

"I, um…"

Before he could finish, the door opened and Daisy walked in.

She was still in uniform, eliminating the idea that she was on a date and raising a dozen other questions. Still,

Daisy was in one piece and appeared fine, which left him more than relieved.

"Aunt D, we're winning," Seth said. A wide grin lit up the boy's narrow freckled face.

"Yes, Aunty D. We're beating Mr. Mitch," Grace added.

When Daisy stared dumbfounded at Mitch, he smiled and concentrated on moving the plastic arrow on the spinner. Now would be a good time to feign nonchalance instead of staring at her like…well, as though it was really good to see her.

"Is my grandmother here?" Daisy asked.

"Alice had another engagement."

"She had…" Daisy looked around. "Wait. Where's PJ?"

"I gave her a bottle and put her down."

"You? You did that?" She uttered a small sound of confusion and turned toward the hall. "Let me put my service weapon in the safe and change my clothes before you explain why you're playing Chutes and Ladders."

When she returned a moment later in shorts and a T-shirt, she glanced around the spotless kitchen. "Did you eat dinner?" she asked the twins.

"Oh, yes," Grace said. "Mr. Mitch made macaroni and cheese. *Real* mac and cheese. Not that icky powdered stuff."

"Uh-huh," Christian said. "Good macaroni."

Daisy frowned. "I like the icky powdered stuff. It's an American classic."

Mitch lifted a brow. "Not seriously?"

"My mother wasn't much of a cook." She looked Mitch up and down. "What's that on your shirt?"

"Where?"

Sam turned in Mitch's lap and pointed a pudgy finger at a smear of something that resembled macaroni and cheese on his shirt pocket, along with an unidentified stain on his sleeve. "Right there," he said.

"Thanks, buddy," Mitch said to the little guy.

"PJ did that," Christian chimed in.

"I'd say 'I see,'" Daisy said, "but I don't." Once again, she assessed the room.

Mitch's gaze followed hers as she looked around the kitchen. "Everything okay? We cleaned up to your satisfaction I trust?"

"Mitch, this is tidier than I left it."

"We helped," Christian said.

Daisy stared at them for several moments as if regrouping. Then she clapped her hands. "How about a cookie for dessert? I made those oatmeal ones. They're nice and soft, and have that yummy lemon icing."

"We already had one," Seth said. He flicked the spinner and began to count spaces.

"Have another. Mr. Mitch is going to take a break with me out on the back porch," Daisy announced.

"I'm about to win," Mitch protested.

Seth and Grace both erupted into laughter.

"It could happen," he said to the smiling faces.

Daisy picked up the cookie jar and tucked it under her arm before plopping four cookies on the table. "Let's go, Mr. Mitch."

He put Sam in the chair he'd vacated before following Daisy, who held a death grip on the cookie jar.

Outside, the setting sun disappeared behind the tops of the orchard trees, and the horizon became an inky highway to a moonless night. But the evening was never a reprieve in Rebel. No, the air remained thick with humidity, and the temperature hovered at its usual summer sweat. You simply learned to tolerate it. Mitch ran a hand over his damp forehead and turned to Daisy.

"Cookie?" she asked.

He held up a hand. "I'm good."

"I'm not." She grabbed a handful and placed the jar on the ground.

"You don't look happy," he observed.

"I'm tired and cranky. It's been a very long day." She bit into a cookie and paused, her eyes round with wonder. "It might be because I'm starving, but this is a really good cookie."

"Almost as good as your pies."

"Thank you." She took another bite. "So you were explaining why you're babysitting."

"Was I?"

"If you don't mind. I mean, not that I'm not grateful, but I am a tad confused."

"Your grandmother mentioned that she was invited to the mayor's house with her friends to watch the fireworks."

"That doesn't explain Chutes and Ladders."

"Seth said you didn't have Monopoly."

"Funny."

"I told your grandmother that I'd stay with the kids until you got home."

"On purpose?" Daisy coughed around a mouthful of cookie.

"Are you okay?"

She offered a furious nod and swallowed. "Who does that? Who volunteers to babysit five kids?"

"Don't you have any people in your life who do things just because they're your friend?"

She narrowed her eyes. "Is that a trick question? Because the answer is obviously no. I had a mother who walked out when my father died. My faithful boyfriend of three years peeled rubber when he realized things were going to get, in his words, 'complicated.' My grandmother is the only exception to the bail when things get messy rule."

"I'm sorry for that," Mitch said. He bit back a commentary on the fact that the MIA boyfriend didn't deserve Daisy anyhow. Instead, he relaxed his now clenched fists and placed them on the rough wood of the porch railing. "You're in Rebel now," he continued. "And your friends here stick around when the going gets tough."

"Why does it seem that you're always the friend who comes to my rescue?" she asked.

Mitch shrugged. "Coincidence?"

Both Daisy and Mitch turned their heads at the song of a barn owl.

Daisy peered into the kitchen window. "What did you put in that mac and cheese?"

"Huh?"

"Look at them."

He followed her gaze. Around the table, Daisy's children were laughing as they continued playing the game. "What? They look like happy, normal kids to me."

"That's my point. They're good kids, but I haven't seen them so animated and happy in a long time."

"Grace and Seth were happy when we were fishing."

"Yes, and the common denominator there is you. You're good with them." A smile touched her lips. "They like you, Mitch."

A warm fuzzy something wrapped around his heart. "I like them too." As the words slipped from his mouth, Mitch considered how true they were. Today had been a very good day. The only thing that could have made it better was if Daisy was with them. He blinked at the realization.

"I can't believe Sam and Christian are still awake," Daisy finally said. "They're lightweights. Two lemonades and a little excitement, and they're out for the count."

"They did fall asleep, and then Seth sent a long ball sailing through a window and they woke up."

"He *what*?" Daisy stepped off the porch and looked up

at the second-story window as though she could possibly see in the dark.

"I've already taped and measured the glass. Then we mowed the yard a little farther back so he can practice without taking out every window in the house."

"I told him to hit the balls in the other direction."

"I guess he forgot."

Daisy shoved the last piece of cookie into her mouth. "You mowed the grass too?"

"We had time on our hands."

She nodded slowly. "Let me see if I have this straight. You babysat and mowed the lawn and made mac and cheese and then played board games. All on your day off."

"I enjoyed it."

"You did?" Daisy clasped her hands together and worried at her lips. "You must think I'm totally irresponsible. But I did text my grandmother that I was running late."

"It's all good." He slid his hands into the pockets of his pants, and stared at the porch floorboards. "I thought you might have had a date."

"Are you kidding me? I have five kids." Laughter bubbled from her mouth. "Not to mention, I look like I haven't had a good night's sleep in a month."

Mitch raised his head and stared at her. Did she not realize how beautiful she was?

Her eyes met his and held for a moment before she looked away.

"The fact remains," she said, "that I owe you an apology. I didn't mean to be so late."

"I called dispatch," Mitch said. "Nothing remarkable happened on your shift."

"Is that what they said?"

"Yes." He looked at her again, waiting for her to explain. This time she avoided eye contact.

"Is there something I should know?" he asked.

"Probably. Let me get the kids to bed first."

The screen door creaked open, and Seth stuck his head outside. "Aunt D, the fireworks are starting. I saw them in the sky."

She looked overhead where the sky was aglow with bursts of color. "So they are." Daisy pulled open the door and held it for Mitch. "Fireworks first, okay?"

"Okay." As he murmured the word, he felt a thick cloud of foreboding settle between them.

"Thank you," Daisy said. "The best view will be from the front porch. Go through the living room."

"Yes, ma'am," he said.

Daisy sat in a rocking chair next to Mitch while the children jumped up and down on the front lawn, yelling with delight as whistles and pops preceded explosive trails of light that lit up the sky over and over again.

In between bursts of light, the children played on the lawn, laughing with abandon.

Daisy never missed a beat, keeping watchful eyes on each child. Mitch couldn't help but admire the woman's love for her sister's children.

"Look at me, Aunt D," Seth called before he somer-saulted across the grass.

"That makes twenty-two. Very nice, sweetheart." She turned her head. "Grace, not so close to the street. Christian, finger out of your nose."

When a loud boom sounded overhead, Sam began to cry. Mitch and Daisy reached for him at the same time.

"Sorry," Daisy mumbled as her arms tangled with his. She cuddled Sam close and placed her hands over the four-year-old's ears.

"You're a good mother, Daisy," Mitch said. "You multi-task like a pro."

"Psh," she scoffed. "I'm working purely on a wing and a prayer."

"Not any different than me fifteen years ago, or my brother and his girls now. Sometimes you just have to step up to the plate and trust the good Lord will teach you how to bat."

"Wait a minute. This from God's personal micro-manager?"

"I was smarter back then."

Gradually, the fireworks began to fade and bursts of light filled the sky with less frequency.

"I guess it's over." Daisy glanced at the kids. "Let me get them to bed, and then we can talk."

"I'll help."

"No, I can't impose on your good nature any longer."

"Daisy, you've been gone for fourteen hours. Let me give you a hand."

She grimaced, as though waging a mental battle with pride and exhaustion. When her shoulders slumped, Mitch realized that he'd won a small and important battle. Daisy was going to allow him to help her.

He stood and reached for little Sam. "I'll take care of Christian and Sam."

"Thank you." Daisy relinquished the child and released a breath of relief.

"You can stop thanking me any time now," Mitch said. "Just tell me where to find their pajamas."

"On their beds. The usual routine. Wash their hands and faces and brush their teeth. We'll worry about everything else tomorrow."

Mitch smiled. Yeah, he remembered the days of usual routines. "I can do that," he said.

"I'll check on the baby, and get Grace and Seth settled in for the night."

"Got it."

Daisy turned away and then turned back. She hesitated, opening her mouth and then closing it. "Are you sure?"

"Yeah. Very sure. I raised my sister and brothers. This will be like old times."

"That might not be a good thing."

"The point is, I can do it with my eyes closed."

"All right then." Daisy nodded. "Seth, Grace, Christian, Sam. Tell Mr. Mitch thank you."

"Thank you, Mr. Mitch," they said in unison.

Christian and Sam were half asleep before their heads hit the pillow. Mitch stood in the doorway, watching both of them for a moment, his mind tumbling back to nights where he stood at the foot of Levi's and Kate's beds as they slept, praying the Lord would keep them safe. Being a parent, even a substitute parent, was the toughest job in the world. One he'd failed at, or Levi would be here right now.

Which was why volunteering at Daisy's house tonight made no sense at all. He should have been running in the other direction. Except it felt right. Too right.

Mitch went into the kitchen and put away the board game. When he finished, he stepped out the back door. It was a moonless night, the sky darker than usual, especially after the recent light show.

The porch door creaked open.

"Sorry it took me so long," Daisy said as the door closed behind her. "Grace wanted to talk. She had a really good time today."

"I'm glad," he said.

They were silent for a long moment, standing side by side on the porch. The night was quiet until the painful shuddering of the air conditioner filled the air.

"What's going on with the AC?" he asked.

"It's still limping along. The repair guy said we'll need a new compressor installed, eventually."

"And?"

"They want to install two units because of the square

footage of the house. Frankly, it's an expensive outlay if I'm not going to be around to enjoy it."

"Why do you say that? You're going to be around. I promised you."

"There's no way you can make that kind of promise, Mitch. We won't know about the county funding until August. I can't sink a couple of grand into a house I might have to sell." She ran a hand over the porch railing. "There isn't a big real estate market in Rebel. This house was on the market for a very long time before I bought it. Moving forward, I have to be practical."

"Everything we've done in the past few weeks has been successful. We're well on our way to some impressive fund-raising, and the community engagement is already a success."

"Mitch, I thought you understood."

"I do, but you can't give up now. We only have four weeks left."

Daisy hung her head and closed her eyes. "Life should come with one or two guarantees, shouldn't it?" she murmured.

"Hey, hey, I'm sorry." Without thinking he was at her side with an arm around her shoulders. "I didn't mean to stress you."

Daisy turned her head a fraction of an inch and met his gaze. He was close enough to see the dark flecks in her blue eyes. Time stood still between them, and for a moment he allowed himself to imagine the impossible. That somehow, someway, he could have a future with someone like Daisy Anderson.

When she stepped away from his touch, he knew that he really was dreaming.

"It's been a long day," Daisy said. "And I really should tell you about it."

"Okay," he said.

She cleared her throat. "Roscoe fell off the roof of Beep Jeep."

Mitch stared at her. *"Excuse me?"*

"Actually, he didn't fall. He rolled."

"Why was Roscoe on the roof of Beep Jeep?" He fought for calm, working to keep his voice even.

Daisy chewed on her thumbnail. "I spotted the cherub."

"The ten-dollar replaceable cherub?" Mitch scrubbed his face with a hand.

"That would be the one."

"Did anyone see him…roll?"

"No. That's the good news. Plus the cherub is safe and sound."

"What's the bad news?"

"Roscoe broke his wrist. He used his hand to break his fall. That's why I'm late." She swallowed. "He refused to cut out of work early, although he did ice his wrist and took over-the-counter medication until we were off at three."

She met Mitch's gaze. "He even let me drive the rest of the shift."

"Did he get his wrist looked at?"

"Yes. At the end of the shift, he insisted that I take him to Tulsa, instead of Lakeview Hospital, so no one from the newspaper would find out. The emergency department was swamped with fireworks injuries. It took hours to be seen."

"And?"

"And it's a distal radius fracture. No surgery required. Roscoe is wearing a cast for the next six weeks."

Mitch released a long breath. All this for a silly cherub. "How's Roscoe?" he finally asked.

"Resting. That nice pharmacist went into the pharmacy on a holiday to get Roscoe's pain meds. I'll check on him tomorrow."

Mitch was silent for a moment. "Why wasn't this in your report?"

"You read the report?"

"I told you, I called dispatch." Mitch swallowed. "I was concerned."

She nodded. "We were on break. On our way to the Gas and Go for lattes. Technically, it was not a work-related accident."

"That was Roscoe's spin, was it?"

Daisy studied her sandals with concentrated interest, and slowly raised her gaze to meet his. "No. Henna's."

He blinked. "Henna was in on this too?"

"Henna helped us understand the policy and procedure manual."

"Right. Because there isn't a chapter in there on flying off roofs," he muttered. Mitch clamped his teeth together and took a calming breath. Henna knew how he felt about protocol, and still she didn't call him either.

"I want to be clear that this was all me and my partner. I am as complicit as Roscoe. I'm not going to throw him under the bus to save myself. And there's probably something you should know," Daisy added.

Mitch raised a brow. "What's that?"

"I didn't stop him. Well, at first I tried, and then I realized that Roscoe needed to do this." She took a deep breath.

Mitch shot her a questioning glance. "Why? Why did he need to climb on a roof? He could have called the fire department to do that."

"Roscoe wanted to keep the Rebel PD from looking foolish."

Again, Mitch was silent. If there was a silver lining to this tale it was that Roscoe had the good sense not to let Daisy on that roof.

"Did you hear what I said?" Daisy asked softly.

"Yeah. I'm processing."

"I guess this means I'll be riding alone."

"That's not my takeaway, Daisy." Mitch raised his head. "Roscoe has eleven months left, and I'm not sure I can keep him or you in one piece that long."

"You can't protect us." She paused. "Roscoe needs to be able to defend his pride, and we both need to be allowed to do the job we're trained to do."

"I'm not asking you to babysit the guy, but maybe next time you could call me and let me take the bullet instead of him."

"I didn't call you because it was your day off." She released a breath. "Ironic, right?" Daisy pushed back a tendril of hair. "If only you could have seen him. Roscoe was alive. He had a purpose. Maybe instead of protecting the guy, you need to find something for him to do that gives him purpose again."

Annoyance poked at him. Maybe she had a point, but right now he wasn't feeling real objective. He met her gaze. "Telling me how to do my job?"

"I'm making an observation."

"Daisy, I've been responsible for others all my life. I've got a bit of experience," he said.

"I understand. But sometimes protection isn't what people need." She paced back and forth, her sandals slapping against the porch floor. Then she stopped and faced him. "Are you mad?"

"This isn't about being mad." No, this was much more than that. He moved down the porch steps, his footfalls heavy. "I'll see you on Monday."

"Thank you. For everything."

Mitch nodded and kept walking. He released a breath while his mind scrambled to figure out how he was going to keep the people he cared about safe. It seemed every time he thought his plans were working, everything fell apart.

And he couldn't be responsible for losing one more person he cared about.

* * *

"It's raining." Daisy bounced PJ on her hip and stared out at the watery landscape through the kitchen window. The scent of wet grass and clean air whispered through the screen of the open back door. A slight breeze shivered the trees, causing a tiny rainfall to dance upon the glass. There was something cleansing about rain, reminding her of starting over and second chances. She rolled her eyes at the irony. This was the background music of her life lately.

When a small plop-plop sounded, followed by another, Daisy whirled around, searching for the source.

"No. No. No." Drops of moisture landed in a puddle on the stove. Daisy pulled a bowl from the cupboard and set it on a burner beneath the drips. When she turned, a splash of water hit her face. PJ laughed as Daisy jostled the baby, while she scrambled to grab a second bowl from the cupboard and place it on the counter. When drops started in a third location, she looked up and confirmed the truth. A wet ceiling, which meant a leaky roof. Because that was what she needed on top of everything else.

How would she bake pies if the kitchen flooded?

"Oh, my, dear. That's not good."

Daisy turned at the sound of her grandmother, who stood in the doorway wearing a sleepy smile and bunny slippers as her gaze assessed the ceiling.

"And the air conditioner died last night," Daisy said flatly. "Fortunately, the kids are still sleeping."

"I'm almost afraid to ask. Does the coffeemaker still work?"

"Yes. It's a fresh pot."

"Wonderful."

"Gran, I don't know how you manage to stay calm through everything."

"What are my choices? Worry doesn't move God. So what's the point?" Her grandmother placed a worn leather-bound Bible on the table. *"'Be careful for nothing; but in everything by prayer and supplication with thanksgiving let your requests be made known unto God.'"* She grinned. "I do so enjoy coffee with my morning supplication."

"I know you're right. However, those ominous dark clouds keep taunting me."

"Isn't this unusual weather for July in Oklahoma? I heard that August is more likely to have rain here."

"Who knows? Four days in a row. This has to be some sort of record. I'm thinking it might be time to consider an arc."

Her grandmother laughed as she reached into the cupboard for a mug. "Aren't you late for work?"

"I'm waiting for a call back from the HVAC guy, but his office wasn't hopeful. They tell me he's swamped. Pun intended." She looked at her grandmother. "And that means with the rain, you're stuck inside a hot house with five kids."

"It's fine. We have plenty of Popsicles, and for some reason they're really into Chutes and Ladders right now."

Daisy chuckled, and immediately an image of Mitch at her kitchen table surrounded by children flashed through her mind. She'd been thinking about that sight since Thursday night.

"What about you, sweetie? Did you sleep at all? You put your fan in Seth's room."

"I'll be fine. It's only an eight-hour shift. Although without Roscoe to keep me on my toes, I'll definitely need more caffeine."

"The kids keep telling me they had a great time with Mitch the other night," her grandmother mused.

"Uh-huh," Daisy said. She did not want to think about how disappointed her boss was with her on top of all the other issues hammering inside her head. No, she'd already lost enough sleep thanks to the heat and thinking about Mitch the last few days.

"That's all you have to say?" Alice prodded.

"For now, it is."

An hour later Daisy pulled open the door to the Rebel Police Department.

"Daisy, are you okay?" Henna asked.

"Fine. Why?"

"You always beat me here. I was a little concerned."

"I had to make some phone calls." Daisy glanced around. "Where's the chief?"

"With Roscoe out of commission, he's patrolling."

"Already? No Monday morning staff meeting?"

"He said there wasn't enough staff to justify a staff meeting."

"And Roscoe?"

"He sent him to the community center. The chief said it was time to escalate our efforts." Henna stepped closer. "Any idea what's going on with Mitch?"

"Why?"

"He was in a surly mood. Even Roscoe kept his mouth closed." She shook her head. "I would have thought he'd be happy to hear that the cherub had been recovered before we made the front page."

Daisy studied the duty calendar, not eager to touch that comment. She turned to Henna. "How's Roscoe doing?"

"Are you kidding? Every officer in this department, except the chief, has given him high fives, kudos and invites to lunch and dinner. He's a hero."

"Good. I'm glad."

"So what's it been like driving without a partner?"

"I never thought I would miss Roscoe's random metaphors on life. But I sort of do." She looked at Henna. "Don't tell him I said that."

Henna held two fingers over her heart in a solemn

pledge. "Never." Then she nodded toward the familiar Eagle Donut box on the counter. "Monday donut? It wasn't easy, but I saved you a cream-filled maple bar."

Daisy chuckled. "I appreciate that. Maybe later. Though I will take a fill-up of coffee. My energy level peaked an hour ago. Nine a.m. and I'm dragging."

Henna peered closer as Daisy poured coffee into her travel mug.

"No offense, Dais', but you look rough. Did you get any sleep?"

"Sleep is overrated."

"The kids?" She clucked with sympathy.

"No. The house." Daisy sighed. "It rained last night."

"Indeed it did. A gully washer."

"So everyone keeps saying. The gully washer brought on a roof leak followed by the demise of the air conditioner. I'm waiting on the AC guy, and I don't have a clue who to call about the roof."

"Oh, my. What can I do to help?"

"Pray the rain stops."

"You know what? I'll pray, and then I'll call my uncle. He does construction and roofing. My brothers work for him during the busy season."

"Henna, my budget is very, um, thin."

"You have to get it fixed. They'll give you the Rebel PD discount. Ask Mitch. They did work on his house. They're reliable." Henna pulled out her phone. "My weather app says no rain for the rest of the week, then we have another front coming in."

"More rain?" Daisy's shoulders sagged.

"Not to worry. I'll have my brothers out to assess the damage before you get home from work today."

"How can you possibly?"

"I'm the big sister. That's how. They owe me so many favors."

That evening Daisy pulled into her driveway and gazed out at the gray-cloaked world. Her mind was stuck on a horrible image. Her bank account. She'd told the HVAC guy to go ahead with the air compressors and the extra installation costs. The nest egg she had set aside for emergencies would be depleted in no time.

Add to that the humiliating fact that her boss was avoiding her.

When she'd stopped at the diner for her carryout sandwich, she'd seen him across the street coming out of the Rebel Police Department. He'd averted his gaze and completely ignored her greeting, instead striding up the street and ducking into the Piggly Wiggly. It was possible that he didn't hear her with the trash truck lumbering down the street, but Daisy preferred to err on the side of paranoia. Mitch had dissed her.

It was time to address the issue. She got out of the van and headed in the house.

"Gran, I'm going to change my clothes and take that lemon meringue to a friend. I'll be back shortly."

"Of course. Oh, and Mr. Eagle and his nephews were here to inspect the roof. They'll be starting on Friday." Her grandmother waved an estimate paper in the air. "This is a ridiculously low bid."

"How do you know that?"

"I called around." She smiled. "Do you think I just sit around here all day and look good?"

"Never that." Daisy opened the refrigerator. "Will you be home for dinner?"

"Of course, it's my turn. Macaroni and cheese night."

"Sweetheart, the kids have requested Mitch's recipe." Daisy huffed. "I've been outclassed by my boss?"

"I'm sorry."

"I'll get the recipe or bring home a pizza. Promise."

Daisy headed back toward town. She drove slowly

down Oak Road until she spotted Mitch's silver pickup in the driveway of a small one-story brick home. Her tongue stuck to the roof of her mouth when she pulled up to the curb and parked. She'd never done anything so bold, but she had to make things right between herself and Mitch.

Daisy grabbed the pie box and checked her reflection in the mirror. Henna was right. She looked like a train wreck. There were dark circles under eyes, and her hair was a frizzy halo thanks to the humidity. She clipped it to the back of her head and applied a quick swipe of lip gloss.

Then she froze.

What was she doing?

This was Mitch.

She walked up the tidy cobblestone path to the house. The brick colonial was framed with climbing ivy. In front of the house, pots overflowed with scarlet begonias welcoming guests. This was Mitch's house? Somehow she'd imagined it less manicured and more…rustic.

She rapped on the burgundy door with its polished brass knocker, and it swung open.

"Daisy?" Mitch's dark eyes widened. In a ratty gray T-shirt and a pair of old faded jeans with holes, the man looked really, really good.

This was her second bad idea in less than a week.

He stared at her as an awkward silence stretched.

"This is for you." She fairly shoved the pie box at him, and spun on her heel as cowardice set in.

"Wait," Mitch called.

She turned back.

"Come on in."

"I guess I could." She paused. "For a minute."

Daisy stepped into the house and glanced around. Polished oak floors were the focus of the little house, with a color palette of copper, rust and forest green. The living room held solid, comfortable furniture and a giant showpiece fireplace. The room could easily be in a magazine spread. Not a single Lego, muddy sneaker or broken crayon in sight.

She remembered this. Yes, this was what her life used to be like. Orderly and calm. Now she struggled to find ten minutes of peace in the shower at the end of the day, and a single piece of clean clothing by the weekend.

Her sister, Deb, had always seemed so organized. Daisy sighed. Maybe she wasn't doing this parenting thing right.

"Nice house," she said to Mitch. A total understatement.

"Thanks, I did most of the work myself."

"Your hobby?"

"Sure. I do a little home repair. It's good therapy."

"Therapy for what?"

He lifted a shoulder. "Whatever. Everything and anything."

"I thought you don't have issues."

Mitch narrowed his eyes. "I don't. However, I do sometimes need time to think things through, and working on the floors or painting the bathroom helps." He shrugged. "Besides, I thought I'd flip this house when I finish getting the yard in shape."

A black-and-white cat wandered into the room and jumped onto the back of the couch like a dainty aerialist, purring before she knocked her head into Mitch.

"You have a cat?"

"This is BB. Blind Betty. I'm fostering her."

"Really. How long?"

"Oh, no doubt, forever."

Daisy smiled at the answer.

"That's Mutt, my other foster." He nodded toward the corner where a massive tan dog lay on an oversize pillow bed, snoring.

"Guard dog?" she teased.

"Absolutely."

Daisy sniffed the air, and her stomach growled in response to the amazing aroma floating past her. "What's that smell?"

"Something smells?"

"In a good way."

"Must be the slow cooker. I've got barbecue chicken in there."

"Slow cooker. That's genius. I have to remember that." She did a sweep of the room and shook her head. "I have to tell you this is all so…"

"So what?"

"Domestic."

Mitch laughed. "Sorry to disappoint."

"Oh, I'm not disappointed. However, it's obvious I profiled you, and I am thoroughly ashamed of myself."

"Didn't I do that on your first day on the job?"

Daisy jerked back slightly at the words. "Why, yes, you did."

"Maybe we're both evolving as people."

"I like that and promise to do better in the future."

"Same here." He tapped the pie box in his hands. "May I offer you a piece of the best pie in the county?"

She smiled. "No, thank you. I will, however, take your secret mac and cheese recipe and a cup of coffee."

He chuckled. "I can do that. You want decaf?"

"Leaded is good. I won't be sleeping anyhow."

"Why not?"

"Long story."

"Okay," he said when she didn't elaborate. "Follow me."

Daisy followed him, and paused at a table filled with framed pictures. "Your family?"

"Yeah. Have you met Tucker yet?"

"I have not had the pleasure. His daughters are beautiful."

"And that's Kate and Reece." He picked up a smaller silver frame. "And Levi."

She noted Levi was tall like Mitch, yet slim like Reece. A handsome young man. Her heart clutched at his loss. One she understood only too well. "That's a good picture."

"Yeah. Gone too soon." He nodded and carefully put the frame back on the table. "Let me show you the backyard. Come this way."

Daisy followed him through the kitchen, where he placed the pie on the counter, and into the yard.

Outside the back door, a five-foot-tall cedar fence wrapped itself around the property. Tiny lights were strung around a pergola that boasted climbing clematis with radiant purple blossoms. Wrought-iron lawn chairs with plush canvas pillows surrounded a firepit. Mitch led her to a patio table.

"You're getting the yard in shape? What's there to do? This is amazing."

"I want raised flower beds."

"Flowers?"

"My mother liked flowers. Sort of in her honor. Lilacs and peonies. Fragrance."

She stared at him for a moment, realizing she'd not only put him in a box, she had completely underestimated the man the same way he'd underestimated her. Every single time she thought she had Mitch figured out, he surprised her.

"Have a seat. I'll get your coffee."

"The recipe too. I can't return home without the recipe. They refuse to eat the powdered stuff because of you."

Daisy sat down and relaxed. The sound of running water from a small fountain nearly put her to sleep.

Mitch returned with a carafe of coffee, mugs, sugar and cream on a silver tray.

"Who are you, and what have you done with Chief Rainbolt?"

"Don't let the cowboy hat fool you. My mother made sure I had manners."

"Why do I think there's a story there?"

"There is. A long, boring one."

"I think you said that once before, but I doubt that anything about you is boring, Mitch."

He slid into the chair across from her and poured coffee into two mugs. "I emailed the recipe to your phone."

"Thank you."

"Ah, by the way, Daisy, you were right."

"Of course, I was." She sipped the coffee. "What was I right about?"

"Roscoe. He needed more responsibility. I put him in charge of the community center. Everything from volunteers to setting up the classroom schedules. Never seen him happier."

Daisy did a double take. He'd taken her advice? "That's…that's wonderful."

"Yep. It wasn't easy, but this micromanager is trying."

"And here I thought you were mad at me."

"That's why you threw that pie at me?"

"I didn't throw it. I was nervous." She stared into the depths of the dark brew. "Have you been avoiding me?"

"Yeah. I have."

She raised her head and met his gaze.

"I was annoyed that you figured Roscoe out after six weeks, and I haven't in all these years." He took a deep breath. "I apologize."

Daisy nodded, though she knew there was more going on. Maybe more than Mitch was aware. Still. This was a step in the right direction. He was beginning to let go of the tight grip he had on control.

His gaze was steady as it met hers. "So we're good?" He touched her hand as he asked.

Daisy's heart did a tiny nosedive. Mitch was a nice guy. If things were different and they'd met at another time, would she give in to the attraction she'd tried to ignore since they met? Only a spark, it pushed itself to the front of her thoughts when least expected and threatened to grow with the least provocation.

But the timing was all wrong. She understood that completely. Yet, deep down inside, Daisy continued to hope for something she couldn't possibly have.

Chapter Eight

"I was in Pawhuska this week and picked up an information packet on small business start-ups for you, Daisy." Luna's words broke through Daisy's thoughts.

"Sorry, what did you say?" Daisy stopped wiping the glass counter of the bakery.

"You've been daydreaming all day." The petite chef's eyes sparkled with amusement. "Who are you thinking about?"

"What? No. I've got a lot on my mind." Daisy turned away, certain Luna would see the pink she knew had crept up her neck. How did she know she'd been thinking about Mitch?

"If you say so dear." Luna slid a thick manila envelope across the counter. "This is the small business packet that details the licensing and such, and how to apply for a loan. You'll qualify without a problem."

"I'm not following."

"The bakery. Now that I've seen you in action, I think you should start your own business. Rent the space from me. Be your own boss."

"What?"

"I know you aren't ready to commit full-time, but perhaps you could look through the paperwork and consider one day a week. This bakery pop-up ends in a few weeks. Why not continue? You've got a hungry clientele. After six weeks, you have regulars. Imagine after six months."

"I hadn't thought about it." No, she hadn't dared to think about actually opening a real bakery.

Luna offered a persuasive argument. There was already a loyal customer base and a growing business relationship with the Arrow Diner and Tallgrass Inn, who regularly purchased her pies. She'd learned which customers preferred which variety, and routinely set aside their favorites for them. They returned week after week.

The shop came with basic equipment in the kitchen. Daisy glanced around the space. A coat of paint, a little decorating, including refurbished tables and chairs from the restaurant outlet online. It wouldn't take much, and the place would be ready to go. The thought of extra income was more than enticing.

"I've seen you on Saturdays, *chica*. This is more than a dream. Baking is a calling, and make no mistake, you are called. People respond to more than your pies. They respond to your heart."

A bubble of excitement pushed itself to the surface, and Daisy dared to let herself dream.

"I know someone who will help you paint the place for almost nothing."

"Really?"

"Mmm-hmm." Luna glanced at the clock. "You go ahead home to your family. Roscoe and I will close up. And please, take the rest of the croissants with you."

"We might sell them." Daisy glanced at the tray of golden flaky pastry.

"We sold out of every one of your pies, and we close in an hour. You and your pies are the main attraction. I don't kid myself."

"I'm an amateur. You know that your pastries are amazing, Luna. You've won awards."

"*Sí.* I agree." She grinned. "Pain au chocolat, croquembouche and galette are in demand by the guests at the ranch. Here in town, the natives tell me that my pastries take a backseat to your lemon meringue, triple berry and French silk."

"I feel like I've insulted you."

Luna laughed. "Not at all." She took Daisy's hands. "Again, I tell you, this is your calling. You should not be hiding your light under a bushel."

"Is that what I'm doing?"

Luna offered a slow nod and turned to Roscoe, who stood behind the register. "Am I right, Roscoe?"

"This is a no-win situation for me. I'm gonna keep my mouth shut, and maybe I'll get pie *and* pastries if I play my cards right."

Daisy chuckled.

"It's late," Luna said. "Roscoe and I are going to dinner. We'll handle things."

"Dinner?" Daisy winked at Roscoe.

"Hamburgers and fries, missy. Remember what I told you about being friends."

"Right. Right." She smiled, liking the idea of Luna and Roscoe, two of her favorite people, keeping each other company. "How's the wrist doing?"

"Feeling good." Roscoe proudly held up his bright blue cast adorned with autographs and drawings. "Everyone in the department signed it. I'm thinking I'll keep it when it comes off in five weeks."

"Five weeks. Was it worth it, Roscoe?"

"Yeah, it was. I've got bragging rights forever, and by the time cherub season comes around next year, I'll be retired."

"Any plans for retirement?"

He offered a wistful smile. "This go-round, I'm going to do something creative with my spare time."

"What's that?"

"Who knows? Baking, maybe, or I could dabble in a

pottery class or painting once I get that community center up and running at the beginning of September."

"Good for you." Daisy scooped up the croissants with waxed tissue and put them in a white paper bag. "I'm off. The Eagle brothers are supposed to start on the roof today."

"Daisy," Roscoe called.

"Yes?"

"Never did thank you for being my wingman during our adventure on the Fourth of July." He held up his cast once again. "Or for all you did."

"I've got your back. That's what partners do."

"True that. You need anything, you've got my number."

"I've had your number since the first of June."

Luna laughed as Daisy pushed open the door and started the chimes singing.

There were three trucks in her driveway when Daisy arrived home twenty minutes later. Three trucks on the ground, along with a dumpster. And there were four men on the roof. One truck looked suspiciously like Mitch's. Daisy stepped out of the van, and was slammed with a wall of noise and the thick odor of asphalt. This seemed overkill for a roof leak.

Outside the house, her grandmother stood talking to a dark-haired, stocky gentleman.

"Gran, what's going on?"

"Mr. Eagle was explaining the intricacies of the roof replacement. He's very knowledgeable."

Her grandmother smiled almost coyly. Was she flirting? Daisy's jaw sagged as she assessed the situation.

"Mr. Eagle, this is my granddaughter, Daisy."

"Nez Eagle." He bowed slightly and removed his ball cap to reveal a thick head of pepper gray hair. "Pleased to meet you, Daisy. You work with my niece. She speaks highly of you."

"Thank you." Daisy shaded her eyes with a hand and

looked up at the roof. "Roof replacement. I thought we were fixing a leak?"

"That is the original roof. It's over sixty years old. It would be a disservice if I patched what needs to be replaced. The next strong rain or tornado winds, and your roof would be in Mrs. Shupe's yard down the road."

"I…I…" Before she could respond, Mitch Rainbolt appeared from inside the house. Daisy caught her breath. "Chief? What are you doing here?"

"I was bored, so I thought I'd lift a hammer."

Mitch bored? Not likely.

He adjusted the tool belt on his hips and turned to her grandmother. "Alice, do you want to show me that leaky faucet?"

"Daisy, could you show Mitch? I promised Nez that I would show him the fruit trees."

Daisy blinked, her head spinning. Mitch? Nez? "Where are the kids?"

"There was an event at the Rebel Community Church. They're even feeding them. I'll pick them up in a couple of hours. No worries."

"PJ too?"

"Saylor Tuttle, the pastor's wife, invited PJ. To keep her granddaughter company." She smiled. "It's PJ's first playdate."

"Right." Daisy said the word slowly and met Mitch's gaze.

He nodded toward the house. "The faucet?"

"They're replacing the roof," she said as she followed him inside. "The estimate was for repair work. I'm not sure I can afford—"

"Mr. Eagle donated the labor on the roof job. So you're getting this at rock bottom cost. He'll work out a payment plan." Mitch looked at her, his face serious. "It's supposed to rain again soon."

"Okay. I suppose I don't really have a choice, do I? And what else is going on?" Daisy asked.

"Henna's brother is repairing your kitchen ceiling. Insurance will cover the cost."

"How do you know that?"

"That's how it works. Besides, your grandmother called them. She told me so."

Daisy stepped into the kitchen and stopped. "What were we doing in here?"

"The faucet."

Right. The faucet. That would explain why he was in her kitchen, taking up so much space she could hardly breathe.

"The kitchen faucet." Daisy nodded. "It's really fine. You were here on Thursday. I mean, occasionally those porcelain cross handles come off, and sometimes they leak. Not a big deal in the scheme of things."

She glanced longingly at the coffeemaker. "I could use a fresh cup of coffee. How about you?"

"Sure. I'll take a look at the faucet after."

Daisy sighed, wishing he'd just let that go.

He frowned. "Everything okay?"

"Perfect." She was being churlish, she knew, but on top of days of sleep deprivation, there was now a house full of people doing work that she couldn't possibly afford. Overwhelmed was the theme of the month.

Things were out of control, and she had no idea how to rein her life back in.

Daisy grabbed the carafe from the coffeemaker and jerked the cold-water knob roughly. The handle came off in her hand, splashing water into the sink where it ricocheted against a dish and up into her face. She jumped back, astonished. Still clutching the knob, she blinked through water that dripped off her face.

"Here." Mitch shoved a towel into her hand. He reached

over to move the plate that targeted the water at her. "Maybe I better fix that first."

Eyes laughing, lips twitching, Mitch accepted the knob she held in the palm of her hand. She dabbed at her wet clothes and face, and all but glared. Her expression dared him to laugh out loud. Much to his credit, his restraint remained exemplary.

Mitch turned over the handle in his hand. "These are so old they're back in style again." Then he opened the cupboards beneath the sink and examined the pipes. "You've got a leak under here too."

Daisy held back a maniacal laugh. "Of course, I do. I thought it was the kids spilling water."

"I'm going to have to turn off the water to repair this. You want to fill up that pot before I do?" He motioned toward the faucet where the water continued to run.

"Fine." Head high, she tried to maintain some dignity despite her poor behavior.

"I can't believe Mary Sunshine is cranky. Where'd all that optimism go?"

For a moment she thought she'd imagined the comment. *"Excuse me?"*

"Who are you so mad at?"

"No one."

"So you say."

Daisy turned to meet his gaze as he leaned against the refrigerator and scrutinized her. In return, she searched for a clue to what was going on inside the man's head. The light of sympathy reflected in his dark eyes. Well, she wouldn't have him feeling sorry for her. Needy she was not. If only things were that simple.

"I'm sorry." She took a calming breath. "It just feels like everything is out of control, Mitch."

"This is temporary chaos. Stop fighting. Let people help you."

"Let people help me." She repeated the words like a mantra spoken in an unknown language.

"Lots of dust and noise here. Too many things for kids to get into. Might be a good idea to move you and the kids to Rebel Ranch for the next few days."

"What?"

"It'll be easier on everyone if you and the children aren't in the house while they're working."

"I can't go to the guest ranch."

"I've mentioned that the ranch has quarters upstairs at the main house."

"For VIP guests. I'm not a guest, and I can't afford Rebel Ranch. I've looked at the brochure. That place is pricey."

"Reece wouldn't charge you. Besides, this is only for a couple of days. Three max."

"Three days?" That meant three days of making sure that five children behaved and didn't spill on the nice furniture or break anything.

"Think of the kids. They get to spend time on a ranch. Interact with horses. Reece even has chickens, goats, pigs and a cow or two. The whole experience. They'll love it."

"I don't know, and I don't understand why a few repairs are going to take so long."

"The Eagle brothers are making you a top priority, in between their regularly scheduled customers."

Daisy rubbed her forehead. "I feel like a charity case. An ungrateful one at that."

"Ah, so that's what this is. Pride."

"Probably," she said. "I've been a solo act for a very long time."

"Allow your friends in Rebel to bless you. Let them give back. You've already done a lot for this town. You're here and you care. That makes you part of the Rebel family."

"I've never been part of such a large family. It's been my grandmother and my sister and me for years."

"This is an adjustment. I get that, Daisy. You adopt five kids and an entire town adopts you."

"Exactly."

"Think about Alice. Your grandmother deserves a break. She'd enjoy some R & R at Rebel Ranch. They have a hot tub and all sorts of amenities for the guests."

"Ouch." Daisy grimaced. "You have me there. I'm being selfish. She's been babysitting in an overheated house for weeks. You're right."

"Thank you."

"What for?"

"For not fighting me on this." He pulled out his cell. "I'll call Reece and let him know you're coming."

"Wait. Wait. What about Star and Rascal?"

"I can handle your cats. They can stay at my place."

"You've got all the answers." She stared at him. Every day her life became more and more tangled with his, and she wasn't sure it was a good thing to put all her trust in this one man.

"Daisy? Can we do this?"

She nodded slowly. "Thank you, Mitch."

"No need to thank me. I'm only helping. This isn't saving the world." He smiled. "Cheer up. A few days and things will be back to normal."

Normal? Daisy nearly laughed out loud. She hadn't seen normal in a long time, and she wasn't sure she'd recognize it if it decided to show up.

"Are you afraid of horses?" Mitch asked. He couldn't keep the surprise out of his voice. Horses had been part of his life for so long. Even growing up in a double-wide, horses were always a given.

Daisy avoided his gaze as they stood outside the Rebel Ranch stables. "No. I'm pacing myself."

"Pacing yourself?"

"Yes. I'm acclimating to Rebel in baby steps. I went to the Western barbecue party, and I went fishing. I should get an A for my efforts."

He tried not to laugh. She looked so cute in jeans and a long-sleeve pink dotted T-shirt. He'd insisted on protective clothing, in hopes he could persuade her to get in the saddle.

Daisy wasn't having any of it.

"You're sure you don't want to ride?" he asked again.

"This is Sunday. Your day off. No working today."

"Daisy, horseback riding isn't work."

"It is for me. Reece took Seth and Grace for a lesson. That's enough equine mastery in this family for one day."

"Chicken."

She raised her chin. "Yes, and proud of it. You can't turn me into a cowgirl in one summer."

"I can try. Come on." He inclined his head toward the roughly hewn double doors of the stables, which stood open and welcoming.

"Come on? Where?"

"We're going to say hi to the horses."

"Hi. That's all."

"Yep. That's all."

Daisy lagged behind as he headed into the building. "Are you coming or not?" he called.

"This is the day of rest. I will not be rushed on a Sunday."

Mitch groaned at her words.

When Daisy finally stepped into the stables, she stopped and glanced around with wide-eyed wonder, her gaze moving from the stalls to the overhead fans and the feed sacks. "This place is huge. How many horses are there?"

"I'd have to ask Reece." He paused. "You know to watch your step, right?"

"That was lesson one. Day one." She wrinkled her nose. "I'm getting used to the smell of things too."

"There's hope for you yet, Anderson." Mitch stopped outside the stall of a particularly gentle Appaloosa. "Meet Domino."

Daisy stood behind Mitch. "Is Domino a girl or a boy?"

"Domino is a mare. A female."

"Her spots are beautiful." Daisy glanced around. "Why is she inside when most of the other horses are outside?"

"I brought her in earlier and groomed her in case you wanted to ride."

"I'm sorry you went to all that trouble."

"No trouble. Domino enjoyed herself, and it gave me time to tell her all about you."

"Don't I wish I was a fly on the wall?"

"It's a good thing Domino can't talk." Mitch smiled. The mare might reveal that he'd admitted to being smitten by the strawberry-haired city girl. What else could he call the strange reactions he had when she was around? His pulse skittered and his hands got sweaty. That wasn't normal.

"Hold out your hand and let her get a whiff of you," Mitch instructed Daisy.

She peeked out from behind Mitch and offered Domino her hand.

Mitch could only chuckle. "A little closer."

When the mare chuffed, Daisy jumped and yanked her hand back.

"Aunt D!"

From behind them Seth and Grace raced into the stables. Their faces were bright with a sheen of sweat from adventures, and they were all smiles.

"Look at you two. How were those horses?" Daisy asked.

Grace pulled off her helmet. "It was so much fun. We learned how to groom a horse and had our first riding lesson. Mr. Reece says we're fast learners."

"They are. You would have been proud of them, Daisy," Reece said as he strode into the stables. He offered Mitch a nod of acknowledgment.

"Thanks for taking them, Reece," Daisy said.

"My pleasure."

"Are you going to ride a horse, Aunt D?" Seth asked.

When his small fingers struggled with his helmet strap, Mitch stepped forward and unclipped the clasp for him.

"Thanks, Mr. Mitch."

"Glad to help."

"Daisy, Seth asked if you're going to ride," Mitch repeated. No way was he going to let her dodge the question.

In response, Daisy rewarded him with a pointed glare before turning back to Seth. "Not today. But soon. Very soon," she said to her nephew.

"Mr. Reece says we can ride the horses tomorrow before we leave," Grace said.

"That's very nice of Mr. Reece," Daisy said.

"Do you think we could get a horse, Aunt D?" Seth asked.

"Let me check into that, sweetie."

"Mr. Reece said we could keep a horse here if we get one," he continued.

To her credit, Daisy listened and nodded. In her shoes, he'd be wondering about how they were going to feed another mouth. But she simply offered a serene smile. Yeah, he admired the way she handled the kids.

"Our birthdays are coming up in September," Grace said. "Maybe we can get cowboy hats."

"I'll put it on the list," Daisy said.

"I sure like this place." Grace leaned against Daisy and hugged her. "Thank you for bringing us here."

Daisy blinked and turned her head, swiping at her eyes with a finger. "I'm glad, Grace. I like it here too."

Mitch swallowed past the lump lodged in his throat, and took the helmets from Grace and Seth.

"They can visit anytime," Reece said from behind them.

"Thanks, Reece." Daisy offered him a grateful smile. "That means a lot."

"I think I want to be a rancher when I grow up," Seth said.

"That can be arranged," Mitch said. "Mr. Reece is always looking for hard workers around here."

"You two go get cleaned up," Daisy said. "Gran has a snack for you."

"Mitch, why don't you take the UTV and show Daisy around the ranch?" Reece said. He pulled keys from his pocket, and tossed them through the air to his brother.

Mitch caught the keys. "I'll do that. Thanks, bro."

"What's a UTV?" Daisy asked when Reece left the stables.

"Utility vehicle. Farms and ranches use them. Helpful for simple tasks like getting the mail, since our mailbox is a hike from the main house."

"Do you have a stable for UTVs too?"

He turned and looked at her. "You've got quite the sense of humor."

"Thank you." She double-stepped to keep up with his long strides out of the stables.

"Reece has a couple UTVs parked outside the barn." They rounded a corner, and he stopped.

"Are you okay with riding the UTV on your day of rest?"

Daisy took one look at the bright green vehicle without doors, and a grin split her face. "Of course. This is so much better than horses."

Mitch offered a low chuckle. "Seat belt on at all times. Hands and feet stay inside."

"Yes, sir."

He backed up the vehicle, and headed over the pasture and forage grass.

"It's so green out here. Like an emerald blanket," Daisy said.

"All that rain. Normally this time of year it's dry, with a few tumbleweeds passing by."

"Perfect day, too. Look at that sky."

Mitch did look and Daisy was right. The Oklahoma sky was bright and cloudless. As blue as the blue sage that grew wild in the spring.

"Anyone ever tell you that you drive like my grandmother?" Daisy asked.

"And you sound like my brother Reece." He pointed to a few muddy ruts in the pasture. "You don't have a helmet, so I'm going to take it slow and stick to the trails. We can go off-roading when you have the proper gear."

Her eyes lit up. "I'd love that."

Mitch released a scoffing breath. "Why am I not surprised?"

"I'm all about speed. I used to ride a little Kawasaki Ninja before I bought my hybrid."

He couldn't resist shaking his head at her words. "I would have liked to see that."

Daisy chuckled at his response.

"Look over to the left," Mitch said. "Those are the guest cabins, and past them is Luna's kitchen and the dining hall."

"Tell me about the ranch, Mitch. Why weren't you raised here?"

Mitch hesitated. "It's not a pretty story."

"I'm not looking for a pretty story. You've heard mine."

"Fair enough." He nodded. "My grandfather disowned my mother when she married my father. When my grandfather died, the property was held in a trust to keep my father from being able to inherit. Every time one of us turned twenty-one, we inherited the deed to our portion of the ranch."

"No one lived here all that time?"

"The land was rented out for grazing a few times over the years."

"Did you know your grandfather?"

"Not well enough. Although I'll let you in on a little secret. Around the time Kate and Levi were born, my father was coming home less and less. Both times Mom was in the hospital, Gramps scooped us all up from the trailer and brought us to the ranch for a couple days."

"Did your mother know?"

"Sure. She pretended she didn't, and the old man swore us to secrecy."

"Good memories?" Daisy asked.

"Yeah. It was good. Except for his dogged determination to keep my father off his land." He ran a hand over the steering wheel. "My father was harmless. Just a good old boy who couldn't figure out how he ended up with five kids or what to do with them." Mitch shrugged. "So he walked away."

"That's a very insightful attitude."

"Don't give me too much credit. I spent a long time wrapped in bitterness and anger. Taking care of my brothers and sister helped divert my hostility." He leaned back and stared out at his grandfather's land. "Took me years to understand. Both my father and my grandfather had passed by then. Now I realize that not everyone is cut out for parenthood."

"I'm sorry."

"What for?"

"That you didn't get to have your grandfather or your father in your life."

"I'm sorry too. Mostly it was their loss."

"Why didn't you go to Tulsa?" she asked.

Mitch nearly slammed on the brakes. "Who told you about Tulsa?"

"Roscoe."

"There's a surprise." He couldn't resist a roll of his eyes. "Roscoe has an idea that I'm hankering to leave Rebel. Not particularly true. Tulsa was never a big deal. Fact is, after Levi died, I just wanted to keep the Rainbolts together. It really hit home for the first time since my mother passed that we were all we had. Each other."

Keeping the family together was the least he could do when he'd failed so miserably at keeping Levi safe.

"I understand," she murmured. "Adopting Deb's kids was the only way I could survive the grief of losing her."

"I get that too," he said softly.

When Daisy pushed the windblown red locks from her face, Mitch reached into his back pocket and pulled out a black bandanna. "Here. To tie your hair back."

"Thank you."

"Did you get to use the hot tub or check out the movie theater?"

"Gran and the kids did. I was working on a business plan."

"A business plan? That doesn't sound like fun."

"To me, it is. I'm a spreadsheet and calculator kind of gal."

"A business plan for what?"

"The bakery. Luna got me the paperwork for a small

business start-up. Tomorrow I go down to the bank to chat about a loan. It looks like I'll qualify without a problem."

"Are you leaving the department?" Up to now, he had refused to consider the possibility that Daisy would leave the department. Instead, for the first time in his life, he was playing the optimist and believing their plan for the funding would succeed.

"No. I'm sorry. I wasn't clear. We've established a customer base with the pop-up bake sale over the last few weeks. I'm going to pursue opening a real bakery one day a week. Saturdays. At least that's my plan." She turned to him. "It won't interfere with my job."

"I wasn't concerned. You've already been juggling kids, pies, teaching classes and the bakery. Doesn't sound like this will be much different."

"I'm finally taking a step toward my dreams. That's the difference." She raised her hand. "And can it get any better than Luna for my landlord?"

"I guess not." His gaze landed on her for a moment before he focused on the trail again. "Daisy, you're pretty amazing."

"Amazing, no. However, thanks to you I got eight hours of sleep in a climate-controlled environment last night. I feel positively optimistic today."

He looked at her. She was wrong. Daisy Anderson was no less than amazing. "So this wasn't such a bad idea?"

"I didn't realize how much I needed this time-out."

They were silent, enjoying the ride as Mitch guided the vehicle past the pond road.

"What are those buildings?" Daisy asked.

Mitch slowed the vehicle down until they sat in the idling UTV beneath the shady branches of a redbud, whose heart-shaped leaves filled the tree's graceful branches.

He pointed to the structures. "On the left is the chapel. That flat building is the reception hall, and there's a gazebo on the other side. Reece got this wild idea to use the ranch for wedding venues and family reunions. It's been really popular. Spring and fall are the busiest months. He's booked nonstop. Had to hire someone to handle that side of the business and set up an office."

"I can see why. It's a brilliant idea."

"The fund-raising dinner that's coming up will be held here."

"I thought we were doing tents. Like the welcome barbecue. Do you think enough people will attend to fill a venue of this size?"

"You didn't hear? The dinner sold out. I told Henna to sell more tickets, and got the ball rolling for the ranch's private venue."

Daisy turned in her seat. "Where are you bringing these people in from?"

He chuckled. "They're locals supporting the cause, and the tourist population that's in Rebel through Labor Day. When people see Luna Diaz is involved, the purse strings open up."

"What's on the menu?"

"Wish I knew. Luna's catering company has kept it hush-hush. She's donating her services for the event. We're only paying for the supplies."

"That's generous."

"Luna believes in what we're doing." Mitch inspected the dials on the UTV dash as he struggled with what was on his mind. "Maybe I could escort you and Alice to the dinner. It's coming right up. Two weeks."

"My grandmother is attending with Henna's uncle."

"Oh, yeah? Good for her." He met Daisy's clear blue eyes. "And you?"

"Like a...d-date?"

When her eyes popped wide, he backpedaled.

"Maybe. Or like two people carpooling, since we're obligated to attend anyhow. Whatever makes you say yes."

"Yes."

Mitch opened his mouth, then closed it. "That was a lot easier than I thought it would be," he finally said. "I was beginning to think you oppose me on principle."

Daisy laughed. "That's not true."

"Glad to hear."

"Is Will Needleman going to be there?" she asked. "I mean, to see what the town is doing?"

"Henna had the same thought. She wants to ensure he can give us a good word when the paperwork is turned in on August first."

Mitch drove the UTV slowly around the pond, a safe distance from where a smattering of people sat on the pier fishing. When he offered them a wave, several returned the gesture.

"Good day for fishing," he said. "And look up there in that maple tree. See that eagle circling? I think there's a nest up there. Not something you spot every day."

"Yes. I see it." Daisy nodded and her eyes met Mitch's. "You really love this place, don't you?" she asked.

"The pond?"

"No, the ranch. You're different when you're out here."

"Am I?"

She nodded once more. "Tell me again why you don't work here?"

"I fell into the police department job out of necessity." Mitch closed his eyes for a moment, thinking back to those early days. "I needed health insurance for Kate and Levi. Both of them were rodeoing, and in and out of urgent care." He shook his head and smiled. "Everyone was peddling as fast as they could in those days, but they were good times."

"Do you ever think about leaving the department?"

"Reece is after me to do just that. The business is growing faster than he can manage."

"That didn't answer the question."

"I'm giving it some serious thought, though at this point in my life, change isn't as easy as it used to be." He turned and looked at her. "Why is this so fascinating to you?"

"You're my friend, and I like this little peek into your psyche."

"It's a scary place in there."

"I don't think so at all." Daisy stared at him and didn't look away. Her gaze remained unwavering, which only confused him.

Where had she come from, this woman who could see right through him? He didn't understand what was going on at all. The only thing he was sure of is that he liked how he felt about himself and the world in general when Daisy was around.

Chapter Nine

Daisy stood in the middle of the room, admiring her beautiful kitchen. They were just supposed to fix the roof and ceiling. A week later and she remained stunned by the transformation. The cracked linoleum was gone. It had been replaced with gray-and-white, checkerboard-patterned flooring. The cupboards were painted the palest gray. Even the kitchen appliances had been replaced. A stainless-steel stove, refrigerator and dishwasher stood where her fifty-year-old appliances once were.

"Where are you, Daisy? We have to leave soon."

"Coming, Gran. I needed a bottle of water."

Her grandmother appeared a moment later with her silver hair wrapped in giant pink plastic hair rollers.

"Gran, I told you I'd lend you my flat iron."

"I like my rollers, thank you very much. Now tell me why you're standing in the kitchen staring at the stove when we're running behind. Nez and Mitch said six o'clock."

"I can't help myself. I'm still trying to figure out how this happened."

"Bartering, dear. He and Nez brought in carpenters and a flooring team."

"That's the story Mitch told me too." She frowned. "I'm having a hard time believing they replaced the flooring and put in new appliances for pies."

"Don't underestimate your pies. Besides, once folks heard that you needed help and had five kids to boot, he had to turn down half of the congregation who stepped up to offer help."

"Really? New appliances for pies?"

"Those appliances are used. A donation. They have a ding or two on them," her grandmother said.

"They look new to me."

"Enough. We're going to be late. Let's go get dressed."

"I am dressed."

"You aren't wearing that to the dance, are you?"

Daisy glanced down at her gray skirt and peach silk blouse. "What's wrong with this?"

"You're going to a party. Not a job interview." Her grandmother shook her head. "It's a date."

"No, it's Mitch. We're friends." Even as she said the words, her mind tumbled back to her conversation with Mitch. They'd never really clarified that it wasn't a date. Had they?

"Friendship is a solid foundation for a long-term relationship."

"What does that mean?"

"You heard me." Her grandmother looped her arm through Daisy's and started up the stairs. "Come. We'll find something that says party."

"Party."

"Yes."

Her grandmother searched Daisy's closet, rejecting item after item. "Where's the burgundy dress?"

"Not the burgundy."

"Try it on."

Minutes later Daisy stood in front of the full-length mirror and grimaced.

The dilemma was needing to be taken seriously and wanting to be noticed without standing out. This was why she didn't do dresses. Wearing a uniform to work made life so simple.

Her grandmother stepped back into the room.

"I love that dress."

Daisy shook her head and wrinkled her nose.

"Why not?"

"Gran, burgundy is almost the same as red, and red says look at me."

"This is a party, Daisy. The burgundy dress is very demure, and it says you are a beautiful woman and proud of it."

"I'd rather it said I want to go home and read a good book."

"Nonsense. Now go find that cute little clutch I bought you. Nez will be here soon, and I need to spray my hair."

"You're sure this dress?" she called out.

"Yes. With the strappy heels."

"No. I can't walk in heels."

"The heels, Daisy. And wear your hair down with the pearls."

"Like this is a real date," Daisy murmured. Once again, she tried to wrap her mind around the idea.

"Did you say something, dear?" her grandmother called out.

"I asked how you know all this stuff, Gran."

"I'm old, that's how."

"No, I think you got the style gene, and I got the Glock gene."

Her grandmother's laughter made Daisy smile.

"Grace is fortunate to have you around for advice, Gran. I'm of no use."

"That's not true. You have many talents." Her grandmother entered the bedroom again and smiled. "There now. Look at you. You will leave our police chief speechless."

"That really isn't my goal," Daisy said. She met her grandmother's eyes in the mirror, and she was touched by the love reflected in the blue eyes, so like her own. "You look beautiful, Gran."

"Thank you, dear."

Daisy grabbed the silver clutch from the bed.

"Are the children set?" her grandmother asked.

"Yes. I kissed them all, and they're in Grace's room playing."

"Perfect. The babysitter will be here shortly. She's bringing the pizza."

"Babysitter." Daisy mulled over the word nervously. Mitch was the only babysitter they'd ever had. "Are you sure she's reliable?"

"She's the pastor's youngest daughter home from college for the summer. We can trust her."

"What about first aid and CPR?"

"Daisy, she's studying to be a nurse. It's going to be fine."

"Okay, okay."

"Now go. I'll be along. I thought I heard a knock at the back door. That might be her now."

Daisy made her way down the stairs, only to find Mitch at the screen door. "Mitch."

Hurrying, she tripped and her clutch fell from her hands and bounced on the new floor. She quickly opened the door, her face warm with embarrassment.

Mitch stepped inside, scooped up the clutch and handed it to her. "Daisy, you look amazing."

"Even though I nearly face-planted?"

"I didn't notice. I was too distracted by how nice you look."

"I guess my grandmother was right," she returned.

"Whatever she said, I agree."

"Have you been waiting long?"

"No, not long. Gave me a little time to pace back and forth."

Daisy laughed. "You're nervous?"

"I haven't been on a date since I became chief."

"I thought this wasn't a date," she returned.

"Daisy, you look way too beautiful to be a carpool buddy."

She blinked, blindsided by the compliments and the

way her heart kept bumping against her rib cage. "I, um. Thank you."

Daisy eyed his crisp, blue dress shirt, teal paisley tie and navy slacks. He'd shaved, and yet a slight shadow of beard remained. Without a ball cap or Stetson on his head, she realized how thick and almost wavy his brown hair was. Except this was Mitch, so his hair was trimmed neatly in an effort to suppress any shenanigans. Still, she found herself resisting the urge to touch his strong jaw and smooth the knot of his tie.

"You look so…" Heat warmed her, circling her neck and moving quickly upward, no doubt flaming her cheeks and ears.

"I look so…what?" Mitch leaned slightly closer, his eyes wide with alarm.

Daisy cleared her dry throat. "Handsome," she squeaked.

"Handsome?" Mitch chuckled. "You had me worried there. Although that comment does beg the question— how do I usually look?"

"You know what I mean. I've never seen you so dressed up." She gripped her clutch tightly, and tried to come up with something witty to say that would bridge the awkwardness.

"What's going on in that head of yours?" Mitch asked.

"I'm nervous too. This is even more challenging than the barbecue in June."

"How so?"

"I'm wearing a dress and heels, and there is the possibility I might have to pretend to dance."

"Does it help if I mention you're going to be the most beautiful woman there?"

"Now that is an excellent line."

He laughed. "It's not a line."

Daisy released a small sigh at the words.

A moment later footsteps pounded down the steps, and Seth, Grace, Christian and Sam surrounded Mitch.

"Mr. Mitch," Seth said, "we wanted to see you before you leave."

"How are you guys doing?" When Mitch stooped down on his haunches to hug each child, Daisy nearly swooned. Mitch was the real deal. And in the span of five minutes, he'd smashed through all the obstacles protecting her heart.

"Ladies and gentlemen," Daisy announced, "we have to go. Your pizza will be here soon. Grace, please set the table. Seth, let your grandmother know we're leaving. And Christian, put a movie in for your brother, please."

Mitch held open the screen door for Daisy. "I like your kids," he said as they headed to the truck.

"That's good because they're very fond of you."

"Does that worry you?" he asked.

"That they like you? Not unless you plan on breaking their hearts."

"No, Daisy," he said solemnly. "I would never do that. Truth is, I don't just like your kids. I love them."

"Oh, Mitch." She sighed, relieved at the words. "I'm glad because I'm pretty sure they love you too."

The breeze rustled the trees, and a whiff of something warm and comforting drifted to her. Patchouli and cedar? Mitch had cologne on? She allowed herself to linger in the captivating scent a moment longer before tilting her head back to assess him.

"This is it," Mitch observed as they walked down the drive.

"What does that mean?"

"It means this is the last fund-raising event before we go live with the community center. I'm going to spend next week working on the paperwork for the county. We're nearly at ten weeks."

"Hard to believe. Ten weeks. I feel like coming to Rebel was—I don't know—part of a divine plan. Do you believe that's possible?"

"Sure do," Mitch said, as he held open the passenger door of his truck and offered his hand to help her in.

"Thank you," she said.

Mitch came around to the other side, buckled his seat belt and backed out the truck. "Except I'm not sure the Rebel PD is anyone's divine plan. Least of all, someone like you."

"What do you mean, like me?" Daisy kept her eye on him as she adjusted her seat belt.

He shrugged. "You're sort of like a shooting star. All vibrant, and full of light and energy. Maybe you need to think more about that bakery and less about the police department."

She stared at him for a moment, stunned and dazed by the lovely words. "We spent the summer working to get funding, Mitch. You're going to be down a man if I leave."

"I can always find a replacement." He raised a hand. "Don't get me wrong. I'm not saying it would be easy. Nope. Near impossible to find someone as skilled as you."

"Then why are you trying to get rid of me?"

"I'm not. It's just when you talk about the bakery, you light up. I don't think you realize it. Maybe you need to think about stepping out in faith and chasing that dream."

"I stepped out in faith coming to Rebel."

"Hey, I don't want to ruin the evening. I'm only giving you my opinion. My opinion and a couple of bucks will buy you a fancy cup of coffee at Rebel Roaster. That's about what it's worth."

He put a hand on hers, and she couldn't ignore the effect. What would it be like to have the right to hold Mitch's hand all the time? To have someone who believed in her and supported her dreams?

"You okay?" he asked.

Daisy nodded. "Have you ever thought about stepping out in faith and following your own dream?"

A slow smile crossed Mitch's face. "Touché."

Both of them were silent as Mitch drove them to the reception hall. There was something about this evening that made it a mile marker of sorts. After ten weeks in her new job, the end of summer was right around the corner. The kids would be preparing for school in three weeks. The community center would be open. They'd not only survived the summer in Rebel. They had thrived. All of them.

Up ahead, the lights from the reception hall guided Mitch's truck to the parking area.

"Looks like there are already quite a few folks here," Mitch said as he turned off the engine. "Are you ready for this?"

"Not really. My stomach is doing somersaults Grace would be proud of."

He covered her hand with his big one. "You'll do fine. Truthfully, the hardest part is no one will be wearing name tags tonight."

Daisy turned to him, her mouth open. "I didn't think about that. I hope I don't embarrass myself."

"I've learned a neat trick. Distraction. If someone asks you a question you don't want to answer or you find yourself knee-deep in awkward, tiptoe out by laying a compliment on them."

"Does that work?"

"Every single time." He smiled. "This town has a population of seventeen hundred. I know plenty of folks, but I can't put a name to every face like they expect me to."

"That's a very good idea."

"I do have my moments."

A horn tooted, and Mitch waved at the driver of an oversize black pickup. "That's Tucker."

"Will he bring a date?"

"No. Tucker is probably bringing Gina. She owns the clinic with him. His best friend."

Mitch paused. "Tucker lost his wife right after the girls were born. His world is his practice and his children. This is a rare outing for him."

"That's tragic," Daisy murmured.

"You know what? Let's make a deal to only talk about happy stuff tonight."

"Happy stuff."

"Yeah, for once, I want to forget the past and just concentrate on tonight."

Mitch was right. Grief followed them both on a daily basis. This one night, they could set it aside and be grateful for all the good Lord had given them. Daisy nodded. "I can do that."

She followed his glance out the window. "That's a lot of people walking in."

"Anytime Luna caters, crowds follow. Half the people bought tickets just to see what she's going to serve."

Daisy took a deep breath and chewed her lip as more cars pulled in.

"It's going to be okay," Mitch said.

She turned to him, and he offered a smile that made her forget everything for a moment. "Mitch, your support and friendship mean a lot…"

Daisy paused midsentence, recalling her grandmother's words. *Friendship is a solid foundation for a long-term relationship.* A long-term relationship. The thought both excited and terrified her.

"Daisy, are you okay?"

"Yes. Sorry. Thinking."

"Looked like you were having an argument with yourself."

"Did it? I guess I've got a lot on my mind."

"You sure that's all?"

"Yes. I'm sure."

A lot on her mind. Daisy shook her head once more. Now that was an understatement.

Mitch climbed out of the truck and walked around to the passenger side, where he opened the door and once again offered his hand. "We've got this, Daisy," he said softly.

His lips curved into a smile, and the dark eyes told her that he was there for her. At that moment, Daisy knew their friendship was in danger because there was a very good chance that she was falling in love with Mitch Rainbolt. The thought left her torn between panic and total peace.

Mitch couldn't help but watch Daisy. His pulse jumped every time he did, yet he couldn't look anywhere else. In the dim lighting of the room, it seemed to him that she floated. The deep burgundy-colored dress swished around her legs when she walked, and her hair danced on her shoulders. He could watch her all night.

For all her protestations about being nervous, she was working the room like a pro. She started by thanking every single person for supporting the community center project. Then she thanked those who had participated in the work done on her home.

When Will Needleman appeared with a glass of soda in his hand a moment later, blocking Mitch's view, he was forced to pay attention to his old friend.

"Mitch."

"Will."

"Nice shindig. Not sure why the tickets were so expensive."

"Henna made you buy one?" Mitch laughed.

"Two. She said I had to support Rebel."

Mitch laughed again because he knew Henna had two comp tickets. "That's the funniest thing I've heard all day."

"Glad I could entertain you. I take it your fund-raising is a success."

"It is, along with the initiatives we started for community engagement. Community center opens August first. Be sure to mention that to your politicos."

"Are you kidding? Rebel has become the poster child for civic engagement. A reporter from the *Tulsa World* got wind of what's going on down here. He and a photographer are coming to interview you."

"Are you serious?"

"Sure I am."

"This isn't part of your plan to woo Henna, is it?"

"It can't hurt, but no. Henna told me what was going on, and I mentioned it in a budget meeting. You've generated a lot of interest, all good, for what you're doing here in Rebel."

"Good on the reelection front, as well. Right?"

"I can neither confirm nor deny."

"Right. Well, do me a favor and send that reporter to talk to Roscoe. He's headquartered at the old library building where our center will be."

"I can do that."

"Thanks, Will."

"Oh, and Mitch, I'd say that funding is yours. But don't quote me."

"Trust me, I won't, since you already told me the funding was mine once before."

"You're never going to let me live that down, are you?"

Mitch recalled the pain in Daisy's eyes when she found out, and he shook his head. "Not likely."

Will narrowed his gaze, and he searched the crowded room. "Uh-oh, I better get back to Henna before someone else asks her to dance."

Reece stepped into the space Will had occupied, and placed his glass on the table behind Mitch.

"What's up with Will?" Reece asked.

Mitch turned to look at his brother. "He thinks we're a shoo-in for the funding."

"Great. You deserve it. You're an excellent leader, Mitch."

"Am I? Or are you trying to get me to the ranch again?"

"A little of both. Just take the compliment. It's good news."

"Yeah, it is. Except a funny thing happened on the way to the funding," Mitch mused.

"What's that?"

"Somehow in the midst of all we're doing in Rebel this summer, I forgot why we're doing it and became more focused on what we were doing."

"That's a good thing. It's also a good thing you won't have to let Daisy go."

"It's not really about Daisy anymore. We need the funding, but it's brought the town together. And lately, I've been thinking that maybe Daisy should be reaching for more than a job in my department."

"Whoa. What's going on in your head?"

"I'll let you know when I sort it out."

"Try not to overthink, Mitch. That always gets you in trouble."

They stood together for several moments watching the crowd and listening to the woeful lyrics played by a western band.

"That is one interesting woman," Reece said after a while.

"Who?" Mitch asked, taking a sip of his soda.

A hearty chuckle from his brother came next. "You know who I'm talking about. Officer Anderson. Your date."

His date. Mitch found himself liking the phrase way more than he expected.

"Interesting is a good word for Daisy," he said to Reece. "How'd you know she was my date?"

His brother inclined his head to where Roscoe moved across the dance floor with Luna. "Your senior officer."

"Some things never change. Roscoe should be ticketed for gossiping faster than the local speed limit."

Reece offered a smile at the comment. "Thought any more about coming to Rebel Ranch full time?"

"Yeah, but I'm not sure the timing is right."

"Timing is never right to take a step of faith," Reece observed.

"That I can agree with."

A comfortable silence stretched between them before Reece spoke again. "Heard a story today."

Mitch loosened his tie. "Are you gossiping too?"

Reece raised a brow in an expression of indignation. "It's not gossip. This is news."

"Right. Right. News."

"You want to know or not?"

"I'm not even sure what you're talking about, but feel free to keep rambling."

"Heard from Luna that Daisy is interested in the empty bakery shop."

"That's old news."

Reece shook his head. "Patience. That was my warm-up information. Daisy asked me if I knew someone who could help her with painting and minor reno work on the inside. Apparently, her loan was approved and she's eager to get started."

"Where's this story going?"

"I introduced her to Scott Turner. He does small reno jobs in the area."

"You aren't talking about Smooth Move Turner, are you?"

"Yeah, Scott Turner." Reece looked at Mitch. "That was a high school nickname."

Mitch knew he was scowling, but couldn't help himself. "You have a problem with Scott?"

"I'm just saying that Daisy is one of our own now. If anyone's going to help her, it ought to be someone from Rebel. Scott is in Hominy."

"He grew up here," Reece said.

"He doesn't live here now," Mitch quickly returned, his annoyance growing. As he recalled, Scott Turner was way too tall, dark and handsome. Probably couldn't paint worth a hoot either.

"If you say so."

"What's that supposed to mean?" Mitch asked.

"It means that I'll tell Luna you volunteered for the job. I told her you would."

Mitch blinked. He turned slowly and stared at his brother. "You set me up."

"Think so?" Reece burst out laughing.

"I do," Mitch muttered.

"You fell for it, buddy. Hook, line, sinker and a couple of rubber worms, as well."

"Unbelievable," Mitch said with a laugh. "You're quite the matchmaker, aren't you?"

"I try, since I seem to be able to see what you clearly do not."

"I see more than I let on. Your day will come, little brother. When that happens, I'll be first in line to watch you fall."

"Nope, not me. I let the right one slip away a long time ago. My advice to you is not to repeat my mistake."

At that very moment, Daisy turned her head. The curtain of strawberry waves moved and settled on her shoulders. When she met his gaze from across the room, her face lit up. She smiled, slow and sweet. Mitch found himself stunned silent, his chest tight.

"Would you look at that? That smile was just for you," Reece said. "Your days are numbered. Women like Daisy don't come along in Rebel every day."

"That much I can agree with."

Reece set down his soda and dusted off his hands. "All right then. My work here is done."

Mitch shook his head, his gaze following his brother as he left. When he turned back, Daisy began to cross the room toward him.

"Ready to go?" he asked.

"You don't mind that I didn't dance?"

"Confession. I'm a really terrible dancer. Dancing in public is something that I should avoid."

Daisy laughed.

Mitch placed a hand to the small of her back and escorted her to the double doors, holding them open for her.

Outside he could still hear the soft refrain of the band. He stopped and turned to Daisy. "Hear that?"

"Uh-huh. I love that song."

"Let's dance badly to the music, right out here where no one will know."

Her eyes sparkled with mirth. "I love that idea."

Mitch held out his hand and she placed hers in his. He wouldn't have believed ten weeks ago that he'd be dancing with Daisy beneath the stars to the muted sounds of a band while occasionally stumbling, and then giggling like a kid. He didn't believe it now.

When the music stopped, Daisy smiled up into his face. "That was wonderful. Thank you."

"My pleasure."

They were silent as they walked toward the truck. The evening breeze brought a welcoming warmth after hours in air-conditioning. He unlocked the passenger door of his truck and offered his hand once more.

Settling her inside, he closed the door carefully and got in on his side of the vehicle.

"So what's the verdict?" he asked as he started the truck. "Successful event?"

"Yes," Daisy said. "I even had people asking when we were going to start up our safety classes again."

"That's good, right?"

"It is, and I thought once a quarter would be good for the classes. We can hold them at the community center when it opens in September."

Mitch nodded slowly. "I heard your loan was approved."

"Yes. I should have told you, but it's been such a busy week and I only found out a few days ago."

"Congratulations."

"Thank you." She looked at him across the dark truck cab. "You're still okay with it?"

"Why wouldn't I be?"

"Maybe you think it's a conflict of interest with my day job."

"Not at all. It's only one day a week." He could live with one day a week. Mitch glanced over at her. "So what's next?"

Her voice became excited. "The walls need patching and paint, and I'd like to add shelf space."

"Paint ought to be easy."

"Yes. Luna said she had someone in mind for that."

"You're looking at him."

Mitch pulled the car into Daisy's drive.

"What? No. You've done enough, and I can afford to hire someone now."

"I offered."

He parked and came around to open her door and help her down from the truck.

"When do you want to get started?" he asked.

"Mitch, only if you let me pay you for your time."

"In pies."

"Pies again. I'll need you to make a list of everyone I owe pies."

"Fair enough." As long as Daisy was in Rebel making pies, he'd be a happy guy. Truth was, he'd miss the pies if she left, but he'd miss her more. That was a recent revelation he was adjusting to. He followed her to the back door, where she searched in the little silver bag for her keys.

"Um, Daisy?"

She glanced up at him.

"Tonight was fun, wasn't it?"

Her purse fell to the ground and the contents scattered, rolling over the porch floor. Mitch reached for a tube of lipstick headed for grass.

"Sorry. I've got the clumsies tonight." She had managed to grab everything else and shove it back in her purse before he could. Daisy raised her head. "Found the keys."

"Did you hear me?" He repeated the question.

"Yes. Yes. I enjoyed myself." The keys jangled as she unlocked the door.

He frowned. Daisy's response wasn't quite what he'd hoped for. Now he found himself uncertain of his next step. Shake her hand? Kiss her cheek? What was the protocol here?

"I need to relieve the babysitter," Daisy said, her gaze darting toward the house.

"Sure."

"Um, Mitch?"

"Yeah?"

Her hand lifted, and she lay her palm on his cheek. "You're a good man."

Mitch couldn't move. Couldn't speak while she touched him.

Then, as if in slow motion, Daisy stood on her tiptoes and gently pressed her lips to his. "Good night."

She slipped into the house and Mitch turned away, dazed, feeling like a boy again with his heart on his sleeve. That certainly helped his protocol decision.

She kissed him.

She kissed him, erasing all doubt that he was in love with her.

He stopped walking as the realization slammed into him. He was in love with Daisy and he couldn't tell her, because, well, he was her boss.

He'd broken all his rules. Not only had he fallen in love with Daisy, but he'd fallen in love with every last one of her children.

Chapter Ten

Daisy wiped the sweat from her brow and glanced at her dash clock. One p.m. on a Friday. Soon, the dog days of summer would be over. The heat sizzled and rose in waves from the streets of Rebel. She didn't know hot could be this hot.

Two weeks, and she'd take the kids for the promised excursion to Tulsa to shop for school clothes. Mitch asked if he could go with them. Although she was pretty sure Seth had suggested that, she was all in. She'd been demoted by an eight-year-old who wanted a guy to help him pick out clothes. Mitch seemed eager for the adventure, and even suggested a visit to the Tulsa Zoo while they were in town. Daisy nearly fell over when he brought it up.

She hadn't planned for someone like Mitch to come into her life, but there it was. Every single day she thanked God for his friendship, and whatever dance it was they were doing toward a future.

The man had even stopped by the house the last two Saturdays to help her bake pies. Said he owed it to her for promising so many people. They were quite a baking team, although once she was so distracted by the sight of him in an apron she burned an apple pie.

First time ever. Daisy didn't burn pies, as her grandmother had pointed out numerous times since.

There wasn't even a breeze as she sat in the patrol vehicle at the corner of Main and Second Street, hoping for an uneventful end of shift. Daisy closed all the windows of the vehicle, and turned on the engine to give herself a short reprieve and blast the air-conditioning.

Once again, she checked the clock. The paint she'd ordered was ready. By evening she'd be assisting Mitch as he painted the bakery walls Happy Valley Yellow. She could hardly wait.

When the traffic light changed from yellow to red, car horns blared as a Toyota Camry sailed through the intersection, oblivious to the red light.

Daisy knew she'd jinxed herself with all her thoughts of getting off work on time.

With a sigh, she hit the lights and siren, and reached for her radio button.

"Eighteen-zero-two. In pursuit. Red Toyota Camry. Four-door. North on Main Street. License plate…" She repeated the plate number as she typed it into her laptop with her right hand.

"Roger that, 1802."

The vehicle was compliant and pulled over in response, allowing Daisy to review the results of her database search. Expired registration. Multiple outstanding warrants for moving violations.

"Eighteen-zero-nine is en route." Henna's voice came over her radio. "Wait for backup. Eighteen-zero-nine is en route. Repeat. *Wait for backup.*"

Wait? There was no reason. She could certainly handle a simple traffic stop.

Daisy got out of the car and cautiously approached the Toyota from the back driver's side. The female driver was apologetic and cooperative. Daisy took the license and returned to her patrol vehicle to run the information, then she ordered a tow truck.

Before she could finish her paperwork, another Rebel

PD vehicle appeared, lights and siren engaged. The driver screeched to a halt behind hers.

Mitch.

Daisy got out of her vehicle in time to see him jump out of the Tahoe.

He strode up to her, his eye on the Camry.

"The guy has half a dozen outstanding warrants. You should have waited for backup." His voice was cold, his eyes steely.

"The warrants are on the owner. The driver is clean. I'm going to site her for failure to yield at the red light and impound the vehicle."

"Officer Anderson, I'm not suggesting. I'm telling you that you did not follow departmental protocol."

Daisy flinched at his unexpected tone. "Could we talk about this later, sir?"

"Three p.m. My office."

"Yes, sir."

Mitch got in his Tahoe and left the scene. Daisy found herself rattled by his tone. It was her first serious altercation with him as the Rebel police chief. His reaction was over the top. Daisy kicked at a stone in the road. Everything seemed to be blown out of proportion all because of a simple traffic stop. She knew Mitch and this wasn't going to end well.

It took another hour for the tow truck to show up, and by then she was hot, tired and cranky. A little after 3:00 p.m. she headed into the station. Henna pulled her aside in the back room.

"He's furious, Daisy. What happened?"

"Maybe you don't want to know." Daisy splashed water on her face and redid the clip holding her hair in a tight knot on the back of her head. When she looked at Henna, her friend stood next to the lockers with concern in her eyes. "Hen, it's okay. It was simply a difference of opinion."

"Sure. Okay. Except, um, Daisy I have to tell you. I've known Mitch a long time, and I've never seen him mad. Annoyed, yes. Never mad."

"I'm not sure if I should be proud or ashamed of that dubious honor. Though this really isn't that big a deal." She said the words to reassure her friend, and prayed she'd believe them by the time she got to Mitch's office.

Henna offered a weak smile. "That's the spirit. Go in there with your head held high. You're a good officer, Daisy."

"Thanks, Hen." Daisy stood outside Mitch's office, determined not to be devoured by the lion. Removing her ball cap, she tapped on his door.

"Come in."

Daisy stood at attention in front of his desk as he flipped through a calendar. Her eyes focused on a spot to the right of his head.

"Have a seat, Officer Anderson."

"Yes, sir."

"You broke departmental protocol today."

"Sir, I used my best judgment in the situation knowing the department is short-staffed."

"I'm patrolling, Anderson."

"Sir, you are when you are available."

"All the same. Regs clearly state to wait for backup in a warrant situation." He paused. "Any warrant situation. Period."

Daisy said nothing, fighting the desire to shoot back a dozen responses justifying her actions. Nine years on the job and she'd never been written up. Until now. No. She would not stoop to insubordination.

Mitch got up and closed the door.

"Off the record here, Daisy. You have a family to consider. You can't just go off headlong into potentially dangerous situations anymore." This time he stood as he addressed her, his tone softer.

"Seriously?" For the first time since she walked in the office, she met his gaze. "That's the card you're playing? Everyone has a family. Gallegos, Davis, they've got children. Henna is an aunt. You've got two brothers and a sister. We all have family."

"You're the mother to five kids who lost their parents."

"With all due respect, Mitch. You're letting your past color your decisions."

"Yeah, and I'm the chief so that's my prerogative." He took a deep breath. "I know from your side of the desk it seems like I'm prejudiced against you because you're female. If I'm being prejudicial, it's because of your parenting situation and our friendship. Not your gender. What will happen to those kids if you are killed on the job? Alice is seventy-three. What happens if she's unable to care for them? PJ is a baby. Will they all go into foster care?"

His words slammed into her on a heavy wave of emotion, and she couldn't speak. Every nightmare of every night since her sister died crashed through her mind. The grief of that horrible day when she lost Deb once again came at her like a vicious punch to the gut, and she flinched.

Her brain countered. This was her job. She didn't have the luxury of choices.

Or did she?

They were both quiet for a long time, until Mitch cleared his throat. "This was a bad idea. I can't do this."

"Do what?" she implored, searching his dark eyes.

"Us. I can't do us." He rubbed his sternum with his fist, as though in pain. "I take care of this whole town. That's my job. I don't have room in my life for a relationship. I can't be responsible for one more thing."

Daisy crossed her arms. "I never asked you to be responsible for me. I've taken care of myself all my life. If you recall, I've gone out of my way to not ask for favors or help." She swallowed. "This is why."

"Daisy, it's not you. It's me. If I get distracted, I can't do my job."

She inhaled sharply. "Are you blaming me for distracting you?"

"What I'm saying is that wherever you and I were going, it has to stop." He inhaled. "You didn't follow protocol today, but I am willing to admit that I overreacted."

"What you're saying is that you're afraid. Maybe you need to ask yourself why. Then deal with whatever it is that's holding you back from having a real life."

"You don't get it. Levi. His accident was my fault." Mitch focused on the antique fishing reel on his desk.

"Mitch, your brother was T-boned by a drunk driver. It was an accident."

He jerked his head up to meet her gaze. "How do you know that?"

"I went to the library and looked it up."

"There are details that were not in that article."

"So tell me. Help me understand," she pleaded, unwilling to let him call an end to what seemed only the beginning a few hours ago.

"He needed tires. I should have bought him tires or ticketed him for the bald ones and impounded his vehicle. If I had, his car wouldn't have slid across two lanes after it was T-boned only to be hit by oncoming traffic."

Daisy gasped softly. "That's awful. But none of it is your fault. You can't control everything and everyone around you. You certainly cannot control me."

"Yeah. I know that now. And I can't protect you either. I can't keep you safe, which is killing me."

Her chest tightened at his words. Mitch didn't get it.

There was no way she could make him understand that he had to let go of everything once and for all. She released a pained breath and stood, holding her shaking hands together. "Are we done?"

"Yes."

Daisy felt no satisfaction when she walked out of the office and hung her keys on the hook. Struggling to remain calm, she sat down at the desk next to Henna's and typed up a letter of resignation on the computer. She hit print and signed it. Then she removed her badge and her security card and placed everything on Henna's desk along with her service weapon.

"Give that to the chief, please." Her hand still trembled as she offered the paper.

"Daisy," Henna whispered, her voice anguished. "No. Please."

"Henna, it's not about today. Today was a train wreck that's been waiting to happen for twelve weeks. You know it, and I know it." Daisy nodded toward the back room. "I have clothes in my locker. I'll leave my uniform on the table."

"Then what are you going to do?"

"I'm going to pick up paint at the hardware store."

An hour later, Daisy sat in the dark bakery looking out at the world and wondering how she got to this place. She was the mother of five, in love with a man who didn't have room in his heart for her or her family, because his past had hijacked all the space.

Daisy glanced around the shop. Cans of paint were stacked on top of a drop cloth, along with paint trays, rollers and brushes. A ladder leaned against the wall. This should be a happy day. She was about to put into motion what she'd dreamed of for a very long time. Instead, morose was the only word that described her current mood.

The irony was that Mitch was probably right, although today she wouldn't admit it.

She should have waited for backup today. Why didn't she?

Maybe she felt she had something to prove. Her pride had stood between her and making the right decision. Both she and Mitch were wrong, and that left them at the end of the day with nothing.

The other ugly truth was that Deb's kids *had* been through enough. All she really wanted was to provide a future for them. A future where they could forget their painful memories and simply be kids.

Sure, every day was a risk. There were no guarantees, but at the very least she could get into a line of work that was not on the list of the top ten most dangerous job sectors.

She wasn't locked into law enforcement. For her, it was only a job. A job she'd held as a tribute to her father. Leaving the uniform behind was her decision to make. Not Mitch's.

Did she have the courage to follow through and open the bakery full time? There wasn't a choice anymore. She closed her eyes and said a prayer of thanks, and then pulled out her phone and called her favorite chef. "Luna, I want to negotiate the lease on the bakery. I'm going to open it full time. I'm thinking about an option to buy the building. Call me when you get this message."

Daisy ended the call and stood. The shop wasn't going to paint itself, and the walls didn't care that she had a broken heart.

"Chief?"

"Yeah?" Mitch looked up at Henna from the stack of paperwork.

"Good news." She slid an envelope on his desk. "The

check from the county arrived today. We have the funding."

Mitch glanced at the envelope. "Kind of fast, isn't it?"

"Will said there was no competition. Oh, and the county wants to do an official opening of the community center on Labor Day so they can coordinate press coverage and all."

"Let the mayor handle that." He couldn't work up enthusiasm. Twelve weeks later and none of it mattered anymore if he couldn't celebrate this victory with Daisy and her children.

When he looked up, Henna still stood at his desk. Right behind her, Roscoe leaned against the doorjamb wearing a scowl along with his neon-blue short cast.

Henna cleared her throat. "You should see this." She handed him a piece of paper.

Mitch skimmed the letter, knowing what was coming, yet his stomach was still queasy by the time he finished.

"She quit," Henna said. "What are we going to do about it?"

"Officer Anderson and I had a difference of opinion on departmental regs." Mitch paused. "Nothing to do about it."

Roscoe stepped closer. "I've kept my mouth shut around here lately, and you know that ain't easy. But I'm telling you, Mitch, time flies and before you know it you're my age. The good news is that there are some long moments. This is one of them. It's going to determine the rest of your life."

"Cut to the chase, McFarland."

"Don't let it end like this. Go talk to her." Roscoe paused. "This ain't just about the job, boss. You know it and I know it."

Mitch took a deep breath and ran a hand over his jaw. "I'll think about it."

"Chief," Henna began.

Mitch held up a hand. "It's after five on a Friday, and I can't afford to pay overtime. Go home. Both of you. Have a good weekend."

When he heard the door close twice, and he knew they were gone, Mitch got up from his desk and paced back and forth. For the last two hours, he'd been trying to get paperwork done and failing miserably. Daisy would be at the bakery where he was supposed to be painting her walls after work today.

He turned out the lights and slipped out the back door. It took another five minutes of mental battles for him to put the key in the ignition of his truck and head down the street to the bakery. The sky was dark overhead, and moisture spit from the clouds when he got out of the pickup. He kept walking, his steps as heavy as his heart. With each footfall, he was reminded of what he'd done. Pushed away the best thing that ever happened to him.

For several moments he stood outside the bakery beneath the cover of the overhang, looking in as rain began to fall. Daisy sat on the floor with her back to him, carefully painting the trim.

Thunder rocked the air followed seconds later by a lightning arc overhead. Startled, she dropped the brush. Then she straightened and turned, and her eyes met his through the glass.

Mitch opened the door, and the chimes laughed at him. "I thought I was going to paint," he said.

"Not necessary." The words were curt and detached. She faced the wall again, carefully wiping off a splash of paint caused by dropping the brush.

"You quit the PD because of my high-handedness?" The words were out there before he could find a better way to open the discussion.

Daisy got to her feet. She wiped her hands on a rag, and then faced him with weary eyes.

"The sad truth is that I think I'm in love with you."

Hot pain sliced through him at her words. Daisy loved him, and he'd destroyed everything.

"Unfortunately," she continued, "I want... I need what you can't give me. Someone who is willing to let me fall but will be there to pick me up when—and if—I ask him to. Not a man who's going to spend all his time worrying and trying to protect me from the world. That isn't living. For either of us."

He drew a shaky breath. "Daisy, I can't help it if I worry."

Seconds ticked by as she seemed to consider his words.

"Mitch, you can't bring back your mom or Levi. And you can't control everything around you. Bad stuff is still going to happen. The thing is, this world is a better place because of you, only you don't know that. You're blinded by the past and your fears. It's more than time to turn things over to the Lord. You get to have a life."

Daisy was silent for a moment. "You know," she said softly, "I wanted to believe that somehow, with all the chaos in our lives, you and I were on the way to carving out a niche of our own and that maybe somewhere down the line, we might have a future together."

She closed her eyes and opened them, and he'd never seen her look so miserable.

"Today I realized that nothing has changed in twelve weeks. You still have a tight grip on everything. There's no place for me or the kids in your world the way it is. Maybe if you get rid of some of the stuff that doesn't belong to you, you'll have room for us."

"You're wrong, Daisy." He murmured the words knowing they were too little. Too late.

Mitch walked away, the deep ache in his chest overwhelming. He got in his truck, gripped the steering wheel and headed to Rebel Ranch. Reece would understand. His brother didn't have a life either. And maybe they'd talk a bit more about working full time at Rebel Ranch. After today, that was an option that was looking better all the time. He'd given Rebel PD his best years. He could walk away with his head high.

As he drove, he replayed what Daisy had said over and over in his head. The pain in her eyes. He'd done that. Again.

How could he let go? He flat didn't know how. Maybe it was time to get some counseling. Talk to Pastor Tuttle. He never thought he was the kind of guy who'd sit on a couch and spew his guts, but he'd do whatever it took to fix what was broken. Whatever it took for a second chance with Daisy and the kids.

From the corner of his eye, Mitch noted a sudden movement along the side of the road. Though the late afternoon was shrouded in darkness from the rain, he could see the shape of an animal.

Deer.

There were two. A doe and her fawn. The animals lurched into the road. Mitch turned the wheel hard to avoid making contact.

A sudden violent lurching of the truck took him completely off guard. Above the din of the rain, he heard a whoosh of air, followed by a *flap-flap-flap* sound.

Panic shot from his stomach to his ears as realization struck.

He'd blown a tire. The front right tire.

The car jerked with swift ferocity, squealing as it hydroplaned across the rain-slick road.

White-knuckled on the steering wheel, he attempted to control the vehicle by turning into the skid as it veered toward the shoulder. The truck slid sideways, then swerved into a crazed spinout as though he wasn't steering. He struggled to keep the pickup out of the ditch, and came directly into contact with a tree. The airbags deployed, then the truck spun sideways only to hit something. The grinding sound of metal against metal filled the air. Then everything was silent except the drumming of rain against the truck.

Mitch sat still for a moment, dazed from the impact. Then he evaluated himself from head to toe for injuries. His nose was tender but not bleeding. Probably a minor fracture or bruising. He pulled his cell from his pocket only to drop it between the seats. Working his hand past the seat belt retractor, he unlatched the seat belt. Then he grabbed the cell with two fingers, lifted it out of the seat well and punched in 911.

"Chief Mitch Rainbolt. Rebel Police Department. I'm on Country Road 1803 outside Rebel. I've hit a tree. No, I'll live. Just send a car and a tow truck." He listened to the dispatcher repeat his information. "No. I don't need an ambulance."

Mitch struggled to open his door without success. He leaned back against the headrest and grimaced. There was a whopper of a headache coming on, and his chest hurt from the impact with the airbags.

Levi lost his life in a car accident. So had Daisy's sister and brother-in-law. But he was relatively unscathed. He tried to make sense of that, and kept circling back to the fact that he'd been given a second chance. Somehow, someway, his life had been preserved today, and he'd been handed a do-over. All he could think about as his head and nose throbbed was Daisy and the kids. He had to find a way to make things right with Daisy.

The sound of rain pounding on his truck continued to a steady beat as thoughts tumbled through his mind. He was alive, and he wanted to count the freckles scattered across Daisy's face and tell her he was so very sorry. That wasn't going to happen until he made things right.

On the tail of a crack of lightning that flashed through the sky, the passenger door opened and Roscoe stuck his head inside. Rain and wind snuck into the truck around him.

"Mitch? That you?"

"Roscoe?" He was more than relieved to see the familiar craggy face and bald head. "What are you doing out there?"

"I was on my way to the ranch to pick up Luna. She's got a Shepherd's pie and homemade biscuits waiting for me. Imagine my surprise when I saw your truck."

"Glad you stopped."

"Me too." Roscoe moved a flashlight around the car, illuminating the cracked windshield and the interior. As the beam flashed on the glass, Mitch could see branches from a tree jammed into his windshield wipers at odd angles.

He'd seen plenty of car accidents in his day, and had become jaded about them. Today, however, was a wake-up call. This could have ended badly.

Roscoe assessed him with his flashlight, stopping briefly on his face.

"I'm fine," Mitch said.

"Your nose is starting to swell. You're gonna have some shiners by morning."

"I said I'm fine."

"And I'm calling an ambulance."

"No."

"Sorry, Chief. The regs say I call, and I know how you feel about those regs and following protocol."

"Great, I've been rescued by a guy with 'I told you so' tattooed on his forehead."

"Funny how that works, huh?" Roscoe chuckled "So you gonna tell me what happened?"

"A doe ran into the road. I blew a tire and lost control." He squinted out his window and into the night. "It looks like I went off the road and into a tree, and then the guard-rail stopped me from sliding into a ditch."

"You're taking a beating from women today, ain't ya?"

"Tell me about it."

"In my experience, you're doing something wrong when you keep getting run over. Might want to think about that."

Mitch gritted his teeth at the sage advice but said nothing. That Roscoe was right was an understatement.

"Be right back." Roscoe closed the door and moved around the outside of the vehicle with his flashlight. The bright beam traveled slowly, distorted in the rain, probing the situation, before Roscoe opened the door again. His bald scalp was shiny with moisture.

"Boss, that guardrail probably saved your life. Best I can tell, you hit a tree, then slid into the rail exactly like you said. There's a nice little drop-off you came real close to over there. If your car hadn't settled against that rail, it would have tumbled right off."

Mitch froze at the words, realizing how very close he'd been to disaster. He met Roscoe's concerned gaze. "Why don't you see if you can open my door so I can get out?"

"Oh, no. No way. The guardrail is all bent over there, and practically fused to your door. Besides, it's knee-deep mud. Why, I'd probably slide right over the edge myself."

"Terrific."

Roscoe wiped his face with the back of his hand. "I called the fire department. They'll be here in a jiffy to pry you out."

"I'm going to make *The Rebel Weekly*, aren't I?" In one swift turn of events, his pride and his ego had been smashed. Mitch admitted he deserved the dress down; he just hadn't expected it to arrive so quickly on the heels of his mess up with Daisy.

"You're probably right about the newspaper. Don't see

any way around that," Roscoe said. "Think positive. You saved the deer. You're a hero."

"Yeah, that's not exactly encouraging."

"I hear sirens. Should have you out of here soon."

"Good." He nodded. "Thanks, Roscoe. Sorry about the biscuits and all."

"No problem. You'd have done the same for me, right?"

"Yeah, I would. Anytime."

They were silent as the sounds of sirens got closer and closer.

"Not to go all spiritual on you," Roscoe said, "but sure seems to me like the good Lord was watching over you tonight. You've had a lousy day from start to finish. It could have been a whole lot worse."

Mitch couldn't deny the words. His greatest fears had come to pass today, and yet here he was sitting in the rain with Roscoe on a Friday night. His car was totaled, and he wasn't. Now all he had to do was tell Daisy he was wrong, and pray she was feeling generous about forgiving his sorry self.

Chapter Eleven

Daisy didn't have any problem finding Mitch's room at the Lakeview Hospital. She heard him bellowing the moment she got off the elevator. His lungs were in excellent condition. That was a good sign. She picked up her pace, nearly tripping over her own feet in her rush to see for herself.

Last night was one of the longest of her life, as she found herself on her knees praying that Mitch would be all right after she got the call from Roscoe.

She arrived at his doorway in time to see him sitting in a hospital bed and going toe-to-toe with a petite nurse who refused to stand down. His hair was mussed, and he looked like he had two black eyes. Daisy's heart did its usual flutter, the one she'd stopped fighting. For the rest of her life, her heart was going to dance when Mitch was near. Time to get used to it.

Mitch's eyes rounded, and he stopped talking when he saw Daisy.

"I see you have a guest, Mr. Rainbolt," his nurse said. "We'll be back shortly to take your blood pressure again. The doctor will not release you until he's certain everything is normal."

"I haven't been normal a day in my life," he muttered.

"I guess you're feeling better," Daisy said, knowing that a cranky Mitch was a wonderful thing.

"I hate hospitals." He offered a grimace of annoyance. "Ever notice how everything is 'we' when it's really not?"

She tried not to smile. "I talked to Reece, and he said you're going to be okay."

"Reece went to medical school?"

"I'm not sure about that, but he did call me about the accident." She didn't add that she'd nearly fallen apart with relief when he called to update her.

Mitch only grumbled in response.

"You're in rare form," Daisy murmured.

"I'm wearing a gown. A gown that's too small and has no back side. And people keep coming in here like I'm a stop on the parade route."

Dark eyes intense, he stared at her. "Daisy, what are you doing here?"

"Excuse me?"

"I was a jerk yesterday." The words were a blunt admission.

"You were, but I'm still your friend."

He shook his head. "I don't deserve your friendship."

"I'm here because I care about you. I would have come last night, but my grandmother was in Tulsa with friends and I couldn't leave the kids."

He blew a raspberry. "I had plenty of company last night. Reece and Tucker slept in the room. They snored all night, drank my juice cups and took the extra pillows. I didn't get any sleep."

"That explains a lot," she said under her breath.

"Did you get the bakery painted?" he asked.

Daisy stared at him, taken off guard by the random question. The man had nearly been killed, and he wanted to know how the painting was coming along? Daisy softened her stance as she drank in the sight of him, alive and in one piece. "Not even close," she finally murmured.

"Come here," he said.

"Why?"

"Just come closer."

When she stepped closer to the bed, Mitch reached up a hand and wound a lock of her hair around his finger. His touch made her tremble, and she inched away.

"Hold still," he protested. "You have paint in your hair." Mitch pulled the paint off the strand.

She was close enough to see the bruising under his eyes. "Your eyes look painful."

"A little tender, that's all. I've had worse falling off a horse."

Daisy's phone rang, and she dug it out of her purse. "I'm sorry. It's my grandmother."

"Please. Take it."

"Seth. Sweetie, calm down. Calm down. Stop crying. He's fine. I'm talking to him right now." Daisy held the phone to her chest. "Seth had a few friends over today, and they told him about your accident."

"News travels faster than I thought."

"He's inconsolable. Will you talk to him, please?"

Mitch held out his hand for the phone. "Seth. Yeah, buddy, I'm fine. Someone's telling you tales. I bumped my car trying to avoid a deer in the road, but I'm fine. You should have seen that deer. I wish I had gotten a picture for you." His gaze went to Daisy. "Yeah, I'll be over to see you real soon. Love you, pal. Bye."

Daisy's eyes flew open at the words and she stared at him.

"He told me he loved me lots." Mitch said the words softly. "What was I supposed to say?"

She was so stunned by the vulnerability in his eyes that it took her a minute to respond. "You shouldn't make promises you can't keep."

"Daisy, I never make promises I can't keep. I do love

Seth, and I'll be out to see him and Grace and the rest of the kids."

"When will you be discharged?"

"That is a very good question. I saw a doctor last night. He looked like he was twelve years old. He told me I could go home today if my X-rays came back clear. Haven't seen the guy since."

"There has to be more than one doctor here."

"This is a very small hospital. I specifically told the EMTs to take me to Tulsa, and yet here I am." Mitch shook his head. "I'm pretty sure Roscoe did this to annoy me. Then he told the nurses to pick on me."

Daisy laughed. "Don't they know who you are?"

"Yeah, they do, which is why they're giving me the run-around. They think I'm the guy that fired you."

"What?" Daisy jerked back at the words.

"Yep. Henna tells me she's been fielding phone calls from angry citizens all day. I'm the guy who fired the pie lady."

"No. Tell me you're joking." She tried to grasp what he was saying. The pie lady? She had supporters here in Rebel? The thought bolstered her spirits.

"Sorry, I'm not kidding."

"We have to do something about this situation."

"Again with the 'we'? Daisy, there isn't any we, thanks to my big mouth." He raised an arm, rubbed his eyes and grimaced. "Besides, this ought to be good for your new business."

Her jaw sagged. "I can't believe you said that."

"Me either. I'm sorry." He shook his head. "My only excuse is that the food here is disgusting, I haven't had any sleep, and my chest and nose ache from the airbag."

"Mitch…"

"You should go. I'm too ornery for visitors."

"Mitch!"

"What?"

Daisy sat and pulled her tote bag onto her lap. "I brought you lemon meringue pie."

"Maybe you don't hate me after all." His face softened.

She reached into her bag and put a container of pie and a fork on his overbed table. "How I feel about you has never been the problem."

His gaze met hers, and Daisy's heart stuttered at what she saw there. Deep inside, she knew Mitch cared for her. Maybe even loved her. She swallowed, and held back the emotion threatening to erupt. It wasn't enough.

"After the crash, I sat in that truck glad to be alive and wanting to see you and the kids." He glanced up at the ceiling and then at her again. "I'm sorry, Daisy. Really sorry."

She nodded. "Thank you. That means a lot. But I'm not coming back to the department."

"I get that."

Did he get it? Did he really understand that what stood between them wasn't going to be fixed with an apology?

He opened the pie container and offered a pitiful smile. "This is the best thing that's happened to me since that dinner at Rebel Ranch last weekend."

That evening was special. She clasped her hands in her lap and sighed. Dancing with Mitch in the moonlight was something she'd never forget. Ever.

"So what happens now?" Mitch asked.

Daisy looked up. "Hmm? What do you mean?"

"You and me. Rebel is a small town. Will we see each other?"

"Once my shop opens, you're going to want my pies."

"That's confidence."

She looked pointedly at the empty container.

"There may be some truth in your words." He chuckled.

When Daisy stood and reached over to collect the

empty container Mitch put his hand on hers and held her gaze.

"I realize I have a lot of self-work to do. Tell me that you won't rule out the possibility of us."

"Right now I'm really confused. The only thing I'm sure of is that I have to do what's best for the kids."

"Fair enough."

"I should go." She took the container and slipped it in her tote.

"I'm glad you came."

"Me too."

Daisy walked slowly toward the elevator knowing that whatever happened, Mitch still held her heart, and she wasn't sure what to do about that.

Another perfect day. Any day he wasn't in the hospital was a perfect day. Mitch smiled to himself as he pulled into the driveway of the Kendall house. He corrected himself. It was the Daisy house now. He grabbed the flowers off the front seat of his new truck. Then he paused to say a silent prayer.

This was it, sink or swim time. Fortunately, he was a very strong swimmer.

He rounded the corner and immediately ran smack-dab into Daisy. She smelled like apples and cinnamon and everything he'd been dreaming about for the past week. With a hand on her arm, he balanced both of them.

"Mitch? What are you doing here?"

He grinned and plucked a blade of grass out of her wild red curls and dropped it in her palm.

"I was doing cartwheels with the kids earlier," she murmured.

She ran a hand through her disheveled hair and straightened her shorts and T-shirt. Daisy had never looked better.

"Good to see you, too," he said.

"It is good to see you," she said. Her face pinked, and she licked her lips.

"Why am I here?" he repeated. "Alice invited me."

"Gran!" Her voice wobbled as she called.

Alice opened the screen door. "Oh, no you don't." She scooped up one of the kittens in her arms. "You called?"

"Yes. Mitch is here."

"Mitch! So nice to see you." Alice's face lit up with hope. The same hope he held in his heart for the two weeks since the accident. Every day since his hospital discharge, he'd wanted to come out to the house, but he held back until everything was in order. This would be his last chance, and he wasn't going to blow it.

"Thanks, Alice." Mitch walked up to the porch and handed Alice a bouquet of cornflowers, and then handed Daisy a bouquet of gerbera daisies.

"You are such a gentleman. Isn't he, Daisy?" Alice held the kitten in one hand and the flowers in the other.

"Um, yes. He is." Daisy stared at the flowers as if confused. "Thank you."

"Children, Mr. Mitch is here," Alice called.

The screen door banged open, and all four of Daisy's kids raced out the door. Seth whooped, Grace laughed and Christian and Sam called his name.

"Mr. Mitch, we haven't seen you in forever," Grace said.

"I know," Mitch answered. His heart swelled at the love in Grace's eyes. "And you've grown even prettier."

Seth peeked around the corner of the house and grinned. "Did you get a new truck?"

"Yeah. We'll take it for a spin later."

Christian grabbed Mitch's hand and yanked. "Are we still going to the zoo?" His eager eyes searched Mitch's.

"We'll talk to your aunt about that later. Promise, little buddy."

When Sam tugged on his pant leg, Mitch lifted him

into his arms. Sam planted a wet kiss on Mitch's chin. His heart melted at the sweet, pure love shining on the little man's face.

"I missed you, Sam," he murmured, his voice shaky.

Daisy stood next to the steps watching, her lower lip trembling.

"You okay, Dais'?" he asked.

"I'm good." She clutched her flowers and turned to Alice. "Why didn't you tell me Mitch was coming?"

"I thought I did. Remember when I delivered pies to his house after he got out of the hospital last week?"

"Yes."

"That's when I invited him, and I was sure I told you."

"Is this a bad idea?" Mitch asked, glancing between the women.

"No," Alice said. "As you can see, we've all missed you."

"I missed you all too."

"Mr. Mitch, did that deer punch you?" Christian asked.

"Looks like it, doesn't it? Let me tell you about that deer. She was as big as my truck."

Their eyes grew.

"Did you hit the deer?" Christian asked.

"No. Mr. Mitch said he didn't," Seth said. "I told you that."

"That's right. I stopped so the momma deer and her baby deer could cross the road."

"Why do you have black eyes?" Christian asked.

"This is from walking into my steering wheel. No big deal."

"Children, come and get cleaned up. Dinner is in twenty minutes," Alice called. She turned to Mitch and Daisy. "We're having peaches and homemade ice cream for dessert. Would you two please go pick some fruit for me?"

"Gran," Daisy protested, her eyes filled with thunder.

"Don't Gran me. Pick peaches or no dessert for you, young lady."

"Fine." Daisy carefully placed the flowers on the porch and grabbed a basket.

"Okay if I come with you?" Mitch asked.

"If you want dessert then you better." Daisy swung the basket and strode across the lawn.

"Are we racing?" he asked.

"Oh, sorry. No." Daisy inclined her head to the left. "The good fruit is on this tree down here."

He followed her down the orchard path.

She cleared her throat. "I'm sorry. I didn't even ask. How are you feeling?"

"Pretty good. Sore everywhere, but it was worth it."

"What are you talking about?"

"Near-death experiences are like a kick in the behind."

She stared at him for a moment. "I'm sorry you had to go through that."

"Like I said, I had some common sense knocked into me."

"You had something knocked into you." She clucked. "Those are some shiners."

"It's been ten days. I thought they were getting better."

"Maybe so." She put the basket on the ground and started to examine the low hanging peaches.

"How's the bakery?"

"Good. I ordered the awning." She turned to him. "Navy with gold lettering."

He couldn't help but smile at the excitement in her eyes. "Tell me what it will say."

"Daisy's Pies & Baked Goods." She grinned. "It won't be here for another month though."

Mitch grabbed a perfectly round velvety soft red-and-gold peach. He plucked it and put it in the basket.

"We got the funding," he said.

"Yes. Henna told me. I'd laugh at the irony, but it's not as funny as it might have been last week."

"Daisy, I'm sorry. I've been a complete numbskull."

"Yes, you have." She pulled two peaches from the tree and placed them in the basket. "I thought we already agreed on that."

"Should I throw in narrow-minded and pigheaded?" he asked.

"You know, it really can't hurt at this point."

"I'm leaving the department." He blurted out the words.

"What?" Daisy dropped the fruit in her hand and whirled around to face him.

"I'm stepping out in faith. First of the year, I am gone."

"What is the department going to do without you?" Her blue eyes were round with surprise.

"The mayor will appoint an interim chief, and that person will hire officers to replace you and Roscoe. I've got it all lined up. This wasn't a hasty decision."

"Mitch, I'm speechless."

"You were right about one thing. Life is short. I need to go after my dreams. I'm going to work full time at Rebel Ranch."

"You decided all this since your discharge?"

"Reece has been after me for some time, and suddenly everything fell into place." He grinned. "Or crashed into place. I'm turning things over to God."

"That's wonderful. We both know that God isn't an instant fix. If I've learned anything, it's that He's a healing balm, and healing is a process." Her soft breath caught and she continued. "We've all been through a lot. Grief and guilt aren't easy emotions to navigate."

"Yep. I agree. Pastor Tuttle has me going to a counselor in Tulsa. One day a week for as long as it takes for me to get through this."

Daisy blinked. "Oh, Mitch, I'm so glad you're doing this for yourself."

"It's not just for me. It's for us. The only thing I'm sure of is that I want to go through that process with you. No one else."

"I can't give you any promises, Mitch."

"I'm not asking for promises. I just don't want us to become strangers who pass each other on the street, pausing only to wonder what might have been."

She was silent, her blue eyes hopeful.

"Give me a chance, Daisy. A chance to prove to you that I'm willing to do whatever it takes."

"I don't have a choice, Mitch. I love you too much not to try."

He pressed his forehead to hers. "Daisy, I want to work toward a future with you and Seth, Grace, Christian, Sam and PJ. I want to teach you how to make a proper macaroni and cheese."

She burst out laughing. "Mitch, this is the part where you tell me you love me."

"Daisy, you're the woman I was meant to love. How could I not love you?"

"Oh, Mitch." She wound her arms around his neck and pulled him close.

"I love you, Daisy Anderson," he whispered as he touched his lips to hers. "Forever and ever."

Epilogue

One Year Later

Daisy parked PJ's stroller and stared up at the lettering on the canvas awning. Daisy's Pies & Baked Goods was spelled out in gold lettering against a navy blue background. Would she ever tire of looking at those words when she opened the shop each day?

Today was Saturday and her busiest day of the week. But she'd finally hired help so she didn't have to come in at 3:00 a.m., and she had given up pulling twelve-hour shifts for the time being. While PJ played with a toy in her stroller, Daisy straightened the outdoor tables and chairs, and then bent to inhale the sweet spicy scent of fragrant begonias. She trimmed a few deadheads from the huge pots of the pink blooms that flanked the doors of the bakery.

Her bakery.

It still didn't seem real that a year ago she wondered if she'd get to stay in Rebel. Now it was her forever home.

When she pulled open the door to push the stroller into the shop, the bells sang out a familiar melody of welcome.

The walls of the bakery wrapped her in a buttercup glow. A monochromic mural of daisies covered one wall, its gray tones a contrast to the yellow field flowers.

Gleaming glass counters held domed crystal cake stands filled with her best pies, baked by her newly hired assistant. The room held a few oak chairs and circular tables to encourage customers to relax with their favorite dessert.

"Daisy, is that you?" Luna came out from the back room and glanced around.

"Luna, what are you doing here?"

"Roscoe and I were coordinating the desserts for Henna and Will's wedding reception."

"Luna, sweetie, I need your help," Roscoe called out.

"*Un momento*, Roscoe."

Was Daisy imagining the sparkle in Luna's eyes? She glanced from the back room to Luna. "You and Roscoe?"

"*Sí.*" Luna smiled.

"That's…" Daisy searched for the right word. "Nice. Very nice."

"He makes me happy. Like Mitch makes you happy." Luna looked outside. "Where are the other children? Roscoe said you all would be stopping by."

"With Mitch. He's parking the van."

A moment later the door opened and the bells chimed. Mitch walked in holding five-year-old Sam's hand, with Christian, Seth and Grace trailing behind. All four of the children wore cowboy hats like Mitch's, and their gazes were focused on their new daddy like he was a superhero.

In their world he was.

Daisy's heart swelled at the sight of her husband. Would she ever stop feeling like she was the most blessed woman in the world?

She glanced at her family and smiled. If only her sister were here to see how her children had blossomed thanks to Rebel…and Mitch.

Through her grief and Mitch's they'd been brought together, and now two hurting hearts were healing and their love overflowed.

Mitch placed a gentle hand on Daisy's shoulder and kissed her lips.

"I love you," Daisy murmured.

"Oh, you two. You're still like honeymooners," Luna said. "And look at those hats." She chuckled.

"We stopped at Sheplers while we were in Tulsa this morning."

At that moment Roscoe came out of the back room, readjusting the white canvas bib apron around his middle and brushing flour off his chin. As her new employee, the retired police officer was proving to be a stellar right-hand man at the bakery.

"Are you going to just stand there, or tell us what the doctor said?" Roscoe asked. His gaze went to the large industrial clock on the wall. "I've been waiting for hours."

Daisy placed a hand on her abdomen. "The ultrasound showed twins." She was giddy at sharing the news with her friends.

"Are you sure?" Roscoe returned.

"Yes. It's pretty much foolproof," Daisy said.

"Twins?" Luna raised her hands in a gesture of praise.

"Runs in both families," Mitch said.

"Ha! I was right," Roscoe said. "You've got yourself a softball team."

"Yes. You were right, Roscoe," said Daisy. "What we see in our future is construction. Who would have ever thought a five-bedroom farmhouse would be too small for our family?"

"Congratulations!" Luna said. She reached out to hug first Daisy and then Mitch. "Your cup runneth over."

"Isn't that the truth?" Mitch said.

"I know I've mentioned it before, Chief, but it was mighty nice of you to recommend Henna to fill your position until elections." Roscoe nodded.

"She's earned it. The woman put up with you and me, didn't she?" Mitch asked.

"No argument there. Then again, Daisy put up with us, and now she's got both of us in her life on a daily basis. On purpose."

Daisy smiled at the conversation. "I wouldn't have it any other way."

Roscoe shook his head and offered a lopsided grin. "Seven kids. Boggles the mind."

"Yes. It does," Daisy murmured. She slipped her hand into her husband's, and leaned over to press a kiss to his cheek.

Seven children. A circle of love. And she and Mitch wouldn't be going it alone. They'd face their tomorrows with God's help and the support of their Rebel, Oklahoma, family.

* * * * *

If you enjoyed this story,
don't miss the next book in Tina Radcliffe's
Hearts of Oklahoma series, available later
this year from Love Inspired!

Find more great reads at
www.LoveInspired.com.

Dear Reader,

I'm delighted to begin a new series set in the fictional town of Rebel, Oklahoma. Once a working cattle ranch, Rebel Ranch is now a guest ranch owned by the Rainbolt siblings, Mitchell, Reece, Tucker and Kate.

The first book in this series introduces us to Rebel police chief Mitch Rainbolt and outspoken officer Daisy Anderson. This is a story of heartaches and hope. Like Mitch and Daisy, we too must turn our burdens over to the Lord and receive the healing power of His love.

One of my favorite parts of starting a new series is creating the lovable secondary characters who occupy the pages and our hearts. I hope you enjoy this fun and heartwarming story as much as I enjoyed writing it.

Please do email me and let me know your thoughts. I can be reached through my website, www.tinaradcliffe.com, where you can also find some of the recipes mentioned in the series.

Sincerely,
Tina Radcliffe

COMING NEXT MONTH FROM
Love Inspired

Available March 17, 2020

AN AMISH EASTER WISH
Green Mountain Blessings • by Jo Ann Brown

Overseeing kitchen volunteers while the community rebuilds after a flood, Abby Kauffman doesn't expect to get in between *Englischer* David Riehl and the orphaned teenager he's raising. Now she's determined to bring them closer together...but could Abby be the missing ingredient to this makeshift family?

THE AMISH NURSE'S SUITOR
Amish of Serenity Ridge • by Carrie Lighte

Rachel Blank's dream of becoming a nurse took her into the *Englisch* world, but now her sick brother needs her help. She'll handle the administrative side of his business, but only temporarily—especially since she doesn't get along with his partner, Arden Esh. But will falling in love change her plans?

THE COWBOY'S SECRET
Wyoming Sweethearts • by Jill Kemerer

When Dylan Kingsley arrives in town to meet his niece, the baby's guardian, Gabby Stover, doesn't quite trust the man she assumes is a drifter. He can spend time with little Phoebe only if he follows Gabby's rules—starting with getting a job. But she never imagines he's secretly a millionaire...

HOPING FOR A FATHER
The Calhoun Cowboys • by Lois Richer

Returning home to help run the family ranch when his parents are injured, Drew Calhoun knows he'll have to work with his ex—but doesn't know that he's a father. Mandy Brown kept his daughter a secret, but now that the truth's out, is he ready to be a dad?

LEARNING TO TRUST
Golden Grove • by Ruth Logan Herne

While widower Tug Moyer isn't looking for a new wife, his eight-year-old daughter is convinced he needs one—and that her social media plea will bring his perfect match. The response is high, but nobody seems quite right...except her teacher, Christa Alero, who insists she isn't interested.

HILL COUNTRY REDEMPTION
Hill Country Cowboys • by Shannon Taylor Vannatter

Larae Collins is determined to build her childhood ranch into a rodeo, but she needs animals—and her ex-boyfriend who lives next door is the local provider. Larae's not sure Rance Shepherd plans to stick around...so telling him he has a daughter is out of the question. But can she really keep that secret?

———

LOOK FOR THESE AND OTHER LOVE INSPIRED BOOKS WHEREVER BOOKS ARE SOLD, INCLUDING MOST BOOKSTORES, SUPERMARKETS, DISCOUNT STORES AND DRUGSTORES.

LICNM0320